From Just Enough to Overflowing

Breaking the Tithe Barrier

by
Bob Yandian

Albury Publishing
Tulsa, Oklahoma

From Just Enough to Overflowing —
Breaking the Tithe Barrier
ISBN 1-88008-932-7
Copyright © 1996 by Bob Yandian
P. O. Box 35842
Tulsa, Oklahoma 74153

Published by Albury Publishing
P. O. Box 470406
Tulsa, Oklahoma 74147-0406

Contents

Preface

As my sister and I boarded the airplane for my second trip to Riga, Latvia, vivid pictures of what my wife and I had encountered there a year and a half before began to flood my mind. I decided I had better prepare my sister for what she was about to experience, so I began to tell her all about our previous trip.

My wife, Loretta, and I had been invited by our good friends, Rick and Denise Renner, to come with several other American ministers for a week-long crusade in Riga. A few months before, Rick and Denise had moved to Latvia to teach in a Bible school and hold crusades throughout the former Soviet Union.

When we landed in Riga, the airport was one of the most depressing places we had ever seen. Our spirits could sense the tremendous oppression hanging over the entire area. The walls of the terminal were gray, and the rooms were dark because most of the florescent lighting was burned out. When we left the airport, we were even more aware of the dismal atmosphere covering the city. The once great cultural center of Riga appeared to be still living in the 1940s, with little sign of life or excitement.

Our impression of the city was completely over-shadowed by the impression the people of Latvia had on us, however. Everyone who came to the crusade seemed to be so tenderhearted, but very fearful. They would come to the front of the auditorium to receive from God with expressionless faces. Barely raising their hands, they would look around with blank stares. We couldn't help but wonder if they knew why they were there and what they were asking for.

Their poverty was heart wrenching. No evangelist with any integrity takes money from those to whom he's bringing the gospel for the first time, so Rick took no offerings. Still, they brought what they had, which was flowers. There were flowers covering the front of the stage by the end of each evening.

They wore the same clothes every night, because most of them only had one set of clothes. Rarely did the items of clothing match. Rick said, "When they find a coat, they pick it up and wear it until they find a better one or the one they have wears out. The same goes with every item of clothing they have."

As I shared these sad memories with my sister, I also told her of the great miracles that had taken place. None of us will ever forget the man who had been crippled nearly his entire life, encumbered with leg braces and crutches. The first night of the crusade he received Jesus as his Lord and Savior. The second night he was filled with the Holy Spirit and spoke in tongues.

The third night he was baptized in water with many other converts. And on the fourth night, after hearing the Word of God concerning healing, he threw down his crutches and removed the leg braces. By the end of the service, he was "walking, and leaping, and praising God" just like the lame man in Acts 3:1-8, who was healed by God through the hands of Peter and John.

By the time my sister and I were getting ready to land in Riga, I knew she was adequately prepared for what she was about to see. In reality, however, *I* was the one who was not prepared for what *I* was about to see.

When we disembarked the plane and entered the terminal, we found the airport completely modernized. It was brightly painted and lighted, and we were faced with the counters of every major American car rental company. The whole city had a different feeling to it — brighter, faster moving, like something significant was happening there.

I knew there had been many changes in Rick and Denise's ministry. They were now reaching over 150 million people throughout the former USSR with the gospel on television, had begun pastoring a church in Riga, and had just opened a Bible school, where I would be ministering shortly. Again, I was completely unprepared for what I experienced there.

First, the students in the Bible school were on fire for God. They praised and worshipped the Lord in such freedom, I was convicted in my own heart! But the biggest surprise of all came at the church service that evening. The people were entirely transformed from the last time I had seen them.

There were no more dirty-looking clothes. They were wearing nice clothes. My sister kept asking me, "Where are all the dirty, old clothes, Bob?" I looked and looked and finally told her I couldn't find any. When I eventually found one or two who were dressed like the people I had seen on my first trip, I pointed them out to her so she would have an idea what it had been like.

In sharp contrast to the last time I was there, the auditorium was filled with life and color. The women wore beautiful dresses and the men were dressed in nice suits. But even more amazing was the look on their faces — joy! When praise and worship began, they threw their hands up in the air and sang and danced all over. One man ran around the back of the auditorium, barely able to contain himself.

No longer were the people afraid and intimidated by us. Rarely did we see a vacant look or a blank stare on an expressionless face. After I ministered, they came up and hugged us and wanted to talk. Some of them drew pictures for us, while others tried to speak a little English.

When it was time for Rick to take the offering, I nudged my sister to get ready for all the flowers. Only one person brought flowers. Everyone else threw change into the giant baskets, which were lined up across the front of the stage. The place was so packed, the musicians went through an entire song twice before everyone had come forward to give. This happened for two nights in a row.

I asked Rick how much money the people normally gave. He said, "We get the equivalent of $2,000 American every Sunday." In Riga, that is an enormous amount of money! I was stunned at what God had done in the year and a half since I had been there.

One man on Rick's staff had been able to purchase an older Mercedes automobile. This was so unusual that he had been stopped one night by the local police. They thought someone in such a nice car must be a member of the Mafia! Finally, I exclaimed to Rick, "What has happened to these people? They are completely changed from the last time I was here!"

Rick replied, "They just simply believe the Word of God, and when they believe it, they do it. I don't have to convince them. When I taught them about giving, they started giving whatever they had, which in the beginning was mostly flowers. But they would give to God and trust Him and soon jobs began opening up for them. They slowly began to prosper, and now they're trying to prosper each other!"

The shock of this incredible transformation of the believers in Riga opened my heart to the Holy Spirit in a whole new way. On the first night we were there, He gave me the message that is contained in this book — "Entering the Land of Abundance." I began to teach it to my congregation as soon as I arrived home, and we have witnessed the most exciting financial turnarounds in the lives of our own people! It has been months since I taught this, and still the praise reports come pouring in.

I invite you to open your heart to the Holy Spirit and to God's Word contained in these pages so that you, too, can enter the land of abundance!

Introduction

While I sat and gazed in awe at the shining faces of the believers in The Good News Church in Riga, Latvia, something was really bothering me. I was thinking, "These people have taken hold of something many in my own congregation haven't! My people have heard the Word of God concerning prosperity year after year and some of them still argue against it. If you mention prosperity, some of them give weak excuses as to why they cannot give and why it cannot work for them."

Immediately, I determined to return home and remove all those excuses and doubts.

As I had declared in my heart and from my mouth so many times before, the Word of God is truly God's Word or it is not. It either works or it doesn't work. It's either true or it's not true. The Bible says, "Beloved, I wish above all things that thou mayest prosper and be in health, even as thy soul prospereth" (Third John 2). God wants us to prosper in every area of our lives, and that includes our finances.

If the Word of God concerning the principles of prosperity worked for those hopeless, lifeless souls I encountered a year and a half before in Riga — those who were singing and dancing and praising God with total abandon in front of me now, who were wearing colorful new clothes and prospering financially — then it would work for my congregation.

The same Jesus who went to the cross to provide us with salvation and healing also provided us with financial prosperity — redemption took care of it. The Bible says in Second Corinthians 8:9, "For ye know the grace of our Lord Jesus Christ, that, though he was rich, yet for your sakes he became poor, that ye through his poverty might be rich."

I hear people say, "That's spiritual riches, Pastor Bob." Read the chapter! In fact, read chapters eight and nine of Second Corinthians and you will discover Paul is discussing *finances*. On the cross, Jesus paid the price for our sin, making it possible for us to be born again, reconciled to God, and receive all the blessings that come with being His child. Among those blessings are a divine plan and purpose for our life, health and wholeness for our mind and body, being a part of the family of God, and financial prosperity.

Now "rich" doesn't necessarily mean you're going to live in a mansion and drive a luxury automobile in Beverly Hills — unless that's where you live. "Rich" is relative to whatever area of the world you live. If you are a missionary in the jungle, a good tent and a motorcycle may be prosperity to you. Being rich God's way means obtaining whatever you need to live and to do what He's called you to do — and an abundance over that to bless others.

The ultimate purpose of financial prosperity is to preach the gospel.

Picture a congregation becoming so prosperous that it raises curiosity in their city. Visitors come to discover what that church's big secret of success is, and they find the Lord. This has always been God's most important reason for divine prosperity. He proclaimed it to Israel in Deuteronomy 28:1-14 when He named the blessings which would come upon them if they obeyed His Word. He said He would set His people above all nations of the earth in such a way that all others would know it was He who caused them to prosper and not themselves alone.

This kind of prosperity is not just "getting by." This is abundance.

Abundance is having more than you need, more than you ever thought you would have. In fact, abundance means having so much that you can give to others and meet their needs — which is how the world takes notice and becomes curious about you! You can say to them, "God has caused me to prosper. Don't you want to know Him too?"

But how do we enter into the land of abundance? Is there a gateway we must pass through in order to experience this kind of financial prosperity? I believe there is, because the Holy Spirit pointed it out to me that first night in Latvia. This gateway is the same gateway the nation of Israel had to pass through in the natural in order to enter the promised land. It was a great fortress city called Jericho.

1
Opening the Gate

There is a mighty gateway into the land of abundance, and it is mighty for two reasons: the devil wants to keep us out and God wants us to understand the enormous responsibility we have when we enter in. In the Bible, this mighty gateway is symbolized by the ancient fortress of Jericho.

As we read through the following passage from the sixth chapter of Joshua, we understand how these verses of Scripture describe one of the most dramatic and critical moments in the history of the nation of Israel — passing through the gateway of Jericho into the promised land. *These Scriptures also give us the keys to entering the land of abundance.*

Now Jericho was straitly shut up because of the children of Israel: none went out, and none came in.

And the Lord said unto Joshua, See, I have given into thine hand Jericho, and the king thereof, and the mighty men of valour.

And ye shall compass the city, all ye men of war, and go round about the city once. Thus shalt thou do six days.

And seven priests shall bear before the ark seven trumpets of rams' horns: and the seventh day ye shall compass the city seven times, and the priests shall blow with the trumpets.

And it shall come to pass, that when they make a long blast with the ram's horn, and when ye hear the

sound of the trumpet, all the people shall shout with a great shout; and the wall of the city shall fall down flat, and the people shall ascend up every man straight before him.

And Joshua the son of Nun called the priests, and said unto them, Take up the ark of the covenant, and let seven priests bear seven trumpets of rams' horns before the ark of the Lord.

And he said unto the people, Pass on, and compass the city, and let him that is armed pass on before the ark of the Lord.

And it came to pass, when Joshua had spoken unto the people, that the seven priests bearing the seven trumpets of rams' horns passed on before the Lord, and blew with the trumpets: and the ark of the covenant of the Lord followed them.

And the armed men went before the priests that blew with the trumpets, and the rereward came after the ark, the priests going on, and blowing with the trumpets.

And Joshua had commanded the people, saying, Ye shall not shout, nor make any noise with your voice, neither shall any word proceed out of your mouth, until the day I bid you shout; then shall ye shout.

So the ark of the Lord compassed the city, going about it once: and they came into the camp, and lodged in the camp.

And Joshua rose early in the morning, and the priests took up the ark of the Lord.

And seven priests bearing seven trumpets of rams' horns before the ark of the Lord went on continually, and blew with the trumpets: and the armed men went before them; but the rearward came after the ark of the Lord, the priests going on, and blowing with the trumpets.

And the second day they compassed the city once, and returned into the camp: so they did six days.

And it came to pass on the seventh day, that they rose early about the dawning of the day, and compassed the city after the same manner seven times: only on that day they compassed the city seven times.

And it came to pass at the seventh time, when the priests blew with the trumpets, Joshua said unto the people, Shout; for the Lord hath given you the city.

And the city shall be accursed, even it, and all that are therein, to the Lord: only Rahab the harlot shall live, she and all that are with her in the house, because she hid the messengers that we sent.

And ye, in any wise keep yourselves from the accursed thing, lest ye make yourselves accursed, when ye take of the accursed thing, and make the camp of Israel a curse, and trouble it.

But all the silver, and gold, and vessels of brass and iron, are consecrated unto the Lord: they shall come into the treasury of the Lord.

So the people shouted when the priests blew with the trumpets: and it came to pass, when the people heard the sound of the trumpet, and the people shouted with a great shout, that the wall fell down flat, so that the people went up into the city, every man straight before him, and they took the city.

Joshua 6:1-20

From this passage of Scripture we can see how Jericho was the gateway into the promised land of Canaan. As a border city, no one could enter Canaan except through Jericho. It stood at the Jordan River with its towering walls facing the wilderness on one side and Canaan on the other. In other words, the city of Jericho was the gateway out of the wilderness as well as the gateway into the promised land.

Israel could not go around Jericho, because both the tactical and spiritual importance of this particular city could not be ignored. Jericho was the major city of defense for Canaan, and it had to be conquered *first*. Whenever a nation is preparing for war, they send their best fighting men to the borders, and Canaan's mightiest men of war were in Jericho. They used this strategy to defeat their enemy as fast as they could right at their border. Because of this, they could keep their adversary from entering their land.

Not only were Canaan's mightiest warriors in Jericho, but the thickest wall of any city that existed in the promised land was constructed around Jericho. History tells us the wall was so thick, five or six chariots could race side-by-side on top of it! They had chariot races on the wall just to frighten their enemies.

When the nation of Israel approached Jericho, they were faced with a massive thick wall made of huge stones. They saw giants on the inside who were mighty men of war, and their king was also a fierce man of war. This ancient border city housed Canaan's mightiest forces within a wall that looked impassable. To say Jericho was intimidating to the strongest of armies is an understatement, and Israel was hardly a trained military force.

Nevertheless, as Joshua looked in awe at this fortress of Jericho, the Lord said to him, "See, I have given into thine hand, Jericho." Notice that He used *past tense*. The Lord had already given Joshua the city of Jericho before Israel came near it. In fact, He actually had given it to Israel's fathers *forty years before*. How do we know this? When Joshua sent spies into Jericho, they were taken in by Rahab the harlot, who told them:

> **For we have heard how the Lord dried up the water of the Red sea for you, when ye came out of Egypt; and what ye did unto the two kings of the Amorites, that were on the other side Jordan, Sihon and Og, whom ye utterly destroyed.**

**And as soon as we had heard these things, our
hearts did melt, neither did there remain any more
courage in any man, because of you: for the Lord your
God, he is God in heaven above, and in earth beneath.**

Joshua 2:10,11

Unfortunately, when Moses had sent the twelve spies
into the promised land forty years before, ten of them came
back shaking in their shoes and wringing their hands
because there were giants in the land and the men of Israel
were grasshoppers in comparison. Only two — Joshua and
Caleb — came back saying, "We can take the land because
God has given it to us" (author's paraphrase). Therefore,
Israel wandered in the wilderness for forty years until the
unbelieving generation died and a new generation was
born or grew up. It is interesting to note that, of the older
generation, only Joshua and Caleb entered Canaan forty
years later.

After Moses' death, God appointed Joshua the new
leader of the nation of Israel. He supernaturally led Israel
across the Jordan River and, according to Rahab, now all
the inhabitants of the promised land were the ones shaking
in their shoes and wringing their hands!

The Wilderness of Just Enough

Jericho was the gateway between the wilderness of
Sinai and the abundance of Canaan, but what was the
significance of these two places, if any? I've heard some
ministers teach the wilderness Moses and the children of
Israel traveled through for forty years was the "land of
lack." Then, of course, Canaan was the "land of plenty," the
promised land of milk and honey. However, I believe when
we take a good look at the wilderness, we will see it was far
from a land of lack.

The wilderness was a place where God provided all the
basic necessities of life in the midst of great difficulty, and it

was also a place of preparation for the promised land. The "land of lack" was actually Egypt. In the book of Deuteronomy, we have a passage of Scripture which gives a clear description of Egypt, the wilderness, and the promised land.

> For the Lord thy God bringeth thee into a good land, a land of brooks of water, of fountains and depths that spring out of valleys and hills;
>
> A land of wheat, and barley, and vines, and fig trees, and pomegranates; a land of oil olive, and honey;
>
> A land wherein thou shalt eat bread without scarceness, thou shalt not lack any thing in it; a land whose stones are iron, and out of whose hills thou mayest dig brass.
>
> . . . the Lord thy God, which brought thee forth out of the land of Egypt, from the house of bondage;
>
> Who led thee through that great and terrible wilderness, wherein were fiery serpents, and scorpions, and drought, where there was no water; who brought thee forth water out of the rock of flint;
>
> Who fed thee in the wilderness with manna, which thy fathers knew not, that he might humble thee, and that he might prove thee, to do thee good at thy latter end.
>
> Deuteronomy 8:7-9,14-16

Egypt represents the nonbeliever, who operates under the world's system. The world says they will provide our needs, but they steal from us and abuse us to achieve their own prosperity. That's how the god of this world, Satan, runs things. But when we choose to leave Egypt and cross the Red Sea, which is a type of being born again, we become God's child.

Walking in the wilderness represents spiritual immaturity. As a newborn child of God, we try to understand what it means to be in Christ, what His will for our life is, how to live according to His Word, and how to recognize the voice of His Spirit inside us. During this time of growing up, He will supernaturally supply for us in the same way a mother and father meet all the needs of their young children.

For Israel, the wilderness was such a training ground. Here they learned to trust God every day as He supplied their daily needs. There was a fierce sun during the day, but God sent the cloud to shield them from the burning rays. It was bitter cold at night, but God provided the pillar of fire to warm them. There was no water, so God told Moses to strike the rock to bring forth water. In the forty years they wandered there, none of their clothing, including their shoes, wore out.

Every day God sent manna for their meals. Israel had enough to carry them through each day. In fact, if they tried to collect more manna than they would need for one day, the Bible says it bred worms and stank. They could only have enough for one day. This is a type of Jesus' teaching in what is called the Lord's prayer. "Give us this day our daily bread" (Matthew 6:11). But the Greek actually refers to today's bread. "Our bread the needed give us today" (Berry).

The bread represents the Word of God. While Israel wandered in the desert having every need provided by God, their only task was to collect, prepare, and eat the daily manna which He sent them. The wilderness meant God supernaturally provided just enough for every day. One simple lesson was to be learned: *When you have nothing, God will provide enough to see you through.*

However, God didn't deliver Israel from Egypt, nor did He save us, just so He could provide our needs by doing one miracle after another for the rest of our lives. That's the life of an infant who cannot do anything for himself! He wants us to *grow up* by learning His Word, listening to the voice of the Holy Spirit, and doing His will. Why? Because

He has more for us than the wilderness of just enough, more than living hand-to-mouth day by day! He has great abundance for us, but it comes with great challenges and more responsibility.

As we grow in the Word of God, we will reach a point where we are ready for more responsibility, for greater challenges. We will be tired of having God do everything *for us* and begin to want to work *with Him* to succeed and conquer, showing forth His supernatural power. We will also have a desire to go from having just enough money for every day to having more than enough.

Essentially, what I have just described is a believer who has walked through the wilderness of just enough and grown in God's Word to maturity. They have learned to trust Him for every need on a daily basis, knowing whatever lies ahead, His Word and His Spirit will be there to carry them through to victory. When a believer reaches this point, they are ready to cross the river and take the next step to enter the land of abundance.

Circumcision

After Israel miraculously crossed the Jordan River (Joshua 3) and before tackling the fortress of Jericho, they camped in a place called Gilgal. Gilgal simply means "circle," representing the infinite and steadfast quality of God's Word. Several very important things happened at Gilgal.

First, the Lord commanded Joshua to take twelve stones from the Jordan while it was dried up and build a monument with them. This monument would signify how God was with Joshua as He was with Moses, because He stopped the waters of the Jordan in the same way He parted the Red Sea.

Next, God commanded the men of Israel to be circumcised at Gilgal, which made this place a symbol of

His covenant with them (See Joshua 5). Those who were small children when they left Egypt and those who were born during the forty years in the wilderness had not been circumcised, and it was necessary for them to be in covenant with God before entering the promised land.

Gilgal symbolized God's faithfulness to deliver His people (the monument of stones for crossing the Jordan River) and that His Word could always be trusted. However, with the act of circumcision representing His covenant with them, God was also dealing with Israel in their hearts.

In essence, Gilgal symbolizes where God tests our motives before we enter the promised land. In the natural, circumcision is cutting away the flesh in the most sensitive, private area. By obeying the Word of God in the act of circumcision, Israel was purifying their hearts, surrendering their entire lives to Him, and declaring they trusted Him to keep His Word to them.

Circumcision for the believer today means living by the Spirit and not the flesh by trusting and obeying God's Word.

This is what Deuteronomy 8:18 means when it says, "But thou shalt remember the Lord thy God: for it is he that giveth thee power to get wealth, that he may establish his covenant which he sware unto thy fathers, as it is this day." When we enter the land, we need to remember two things: The Lord is the One Who blesses us, and the purpose of the abundance He pours into our life is to bless others, primarily to get the gospel to them.

We are not entering the land of abundance to heap material things on ourselves or show other people how great we are. There is nothing wrong with having nice things as long as all those nice things don't have us! Riches will never rule our life if we continually cleanse our heart by reminding ourselves that God has trusted us with abundance because He knows we will obey His Word and bless others with it.

Before we enter Canaan, we are to ask the Holy Spirit to reveal any motive that is not in line with God's Word and circumcise it.

I remember when Loretta and I moved out of the area of poverty into prosperity. We always had just enough to get along, lived from paycheck to paycheck, and I had every paycheck budgeted until the year 2,020 unless I died first! I could have told you where everything was going from that point on.

One day we heard about putting the Lord first in our finances, and it was a tough thing to do. We wanted to live in prosperity — who doesn't? — but we had to be circumcised before we attacked Jericho and entered into the land of abundance. We had to say, "The flesh will not reign!" We had to declare when finances began coming in, God's kingdom would remain our first priority. The main purpose of our prosperity would always be to spread the gospel.

As a result, when we decided to obey the Word, took that step of faith, and started giving to God, we could hardly believe what began to take place in our finances. It was like we began moving at an accelerated pace. For example, we had just bought a car and had 36 months of payments. After we started giving to God, we paid for that car in eleven months! What's more, we were able to pay for our next car in cash.

Even then, we had to continue and still continue to camp at Gilgal, to remind ourselves God is the One Who has so generously met our needs and blessed us beyond our wildest imagination. We needed to remember the cry of His heart is to reach the lost with the saving knowledge of Jesus Christ and to disciple them in His Word.

It is in gratitude, as well as obedience, that we give to the Lord. We do not give to the Lord for the cars, the homes, or the money — even though that is a great blessing. Our motive is to give and become successful so we can give even more into the kingdom of God.

At Gilgal, something vital occurs in our lives. We are circumcised in our hearts, making certain our motives are in line with God's Word and our priorities are correct, which purifies us. Anything that becomes purified becomes very strong and formidable. When metal is pure, it is stronger and more beautiful. Therefore, when our hearts are pure, we grow more intimate with the Lord and stronger in faith.

From this position of divine security and confidence, we are now able to take a look at the great wall of Jericho, the wall of our greatest fears and excuses.

Seven Days of Confrontation

After the men of Israel had been circumcised, they celebrated the feast of passover, which symbolized the deliverance of the Lord, and then something very interesting took place. The manna ceased to fall. What did this mean?

God stopped the manna because Israel had come of age. They had left the wilderness of just enough where He had supplied their every need. They had obeyed Him and trusted Him by crossing the Jordan River and having the men circumcised. No longer would they be completely dependent upon Him as babes and young children. They would continue to be dependent upon Him, but as mature believers who would work *with* Him.

From the very beginning, God has sought man to be His partner in ruling and reigning in the earth. I can imagine the most cherished moments for both the Lord and Adam before the fall were the times when they walked and talked

25

together. Now, Joshua and the second generation of Israelites were grown up and desiring to be partners with God in entering the promised land — and so God and man faced the towering fortress of Jericho together.

The Lord gave Joshua explicit instructions on how Jericho should be conquered. It would be accomplished in exactly seven days. On each of the first six days, Israel would walk around Jericho in absolute silence, staring at the massive and intimidating wall at their side. They would then return to their camp at Gilgal. Once they came back to the camp, they could talk. What was the Lord's purpose in giving these instructions?

God wanted His people to confront their worst fears and their excuses for not obeying Him and trusting His Word. He wanted them to walk around the wall every day and stare at each stone as if they were staring at the rent, the car payment, the medical bills, and the insurance payment. He wanted them to see the giants and fierce warriors on top of the wall and confront the depths of doubt, despair, unbelief, and fear in their souls. But that was only the *first part* of each day.

Every day they returned to the camp at Gilgal, the reminder of God's covenant and promises. After circling the wall and looking at the circumstances, they came back to the Word of God and were reminded of His faithfulness as they stared at the monument of twelve stones. For six days in a row they got up, confronted their challenge, and then returned to Gilgal to confront and meditate upon what God had to say about it. They were reminded that the same One Who had dried up the Jordan River for them just days before had told Joshua that He had already given them the city.

On the seventh day, the Lord commanded them to silently circle the city of Jericho seven times and then blow the trumpets and shout. After days of looking first at the impossibility and then the Word of God, they knew God had given them the city. No matter how big the stones, no matter how thick the walls, no matter how large the giants, no matter how trained the men of war were, God was on their side and He was bigger than anything coming against them!

The people of Jericho stood in their own strength, but Israel stood in the strength of the Lord. They shouted with all their might, and the wall fell down flat under the power of God! The city was theirs, and everything had happened just as God had said.

The fall of Jericho reveals a secret of the kingdom of God that Satan doesn't want us to know. When we take the offensive against our fears by trusting in and obeying God's Word, our fears become afraid, our doubts begin to doubt themselves, and the knees of our excuses start to shake! Just as the Canaanites knew God was with Israel, every adversary and hindrance in our life knows prosperity belongs to us. They know the power of God is greater than they are, and their hold on us is only as strong as our fears and excuses to not trust and obey God's Word.

God has given us the city! Although we may not know what will happen tomorrow, we know tomorrow is already ours. Whatever comes against us, whatever great fortress we face, God has already given it to us. Who cares if Satan rears his ugly head and all hell comes against us! Jesus has already promised the gates of hell would not prevail against the Church — and that means us!

Jericho is the Firstfruits

We have circumcised our heart, marched around the wall to confront all our fears and excuses, and given an earthshaking shout. But what, exactly, were we afraid of? What was the reason for the excuses we made? Like the children of Israel, Jericho is ours, but God has commanded all the treasure of Jericho be placed in His treasury.

But all the silver, and gold, and vessels of brass and iron, are consecrated unto the Lord: they shall come into the treasury of the Lord.

And they burnt the city with fire, and all that was therein: only the silver, and the gold, and the vessels of brass and of iron, they put into the treasury of the house of the Lord.

Joshua 6:19,24

Jericho is the first city in the promised land that Israel takes, and the Lord commands them to offer all its riches to Him. They are to purpose in their hearts that the first spoils of battle in the promised land belong to Him.

Jericho represents the firstfruits, or the tithe, which belong to the Lord.

In the wilderness of just enough, as God miraculously cared for us from day to day, and we began to grow in the knowledge of His Word, perhaps we gave to the Lord whenever we felt like giving. As time passed and our ignorance about giving was replaced with the scriptural principles of prosperity, we knew Jericho was ours and it was time to obey God.

Jericho symbolizes the very best and the first of our income, and it belongs to the Lord. Right off the top of everything God blesses us with, we give back to Him ten percent, which is what the word "tithe" means. The firstfruits is literally ten percent of our income.

The moment the tithe is mentioned, most believers' fears and excuses rush in to crush any attempt they make to obey God's Word on the subject. "Pastor Bob, can we get around this city?" No. "Can we just act like it's not there?" No. "But what about my budget? I've already got everything budgeted out. What about my car, the doctor

28

bills, my kids — the unexpected!" What did God have them do for seven days? They were to face their fears. They had to take an honest look at their excuses. They were commanded to walk around that wall in silent confrontation and then go back to Gilgal and meditate on the faithfulness of God's Word.

Fear and excuses are always focused on the future. God has taken care of us every moment until now, but still we entertain thoughts of how our life could fall apart in the next hour, tomorrow, or a week from now. Fear of the future can be compared to the time when the sound barrier began to be tested and was finally broken.

There were many myths concerning the speed at which man could safely travel. People used to say the body could not withstand a sustained speed of fifteen miles per hour for over an hour. They believed once you passed an hour at that pace, your nose would start to bleed and your body would go into convulsions. Of course, when the automobile was invented that myth was soon dispelled.

The barrier was sixty miles per hour for a while, and then it increased until aviators discovered the sound barrier. Every time an airplane would get close to the sound barrier, the plane would begin to vibrate. It was believed if you exceeded the speed of sound, you would disintegrate. However, one day a pilot got in an X-15, surpassed the speed of sound, and discovered it was smooth sailing on the other side of the sound barrier!

Believers have the same experience when they learn about *the tithe barrier!* They shake and quake as they approach it. They vibrate all over as they take out their checkbooks and write that first tithe check, wondering if they will be broke and destitute.

Maybe you took the ride of your life when you tithed for the first time. You came up close to Jericho's wall and backed off, came up close again and backed off, and then one day you finally broke through and gave the ten percent. To your amazement and delight, a great supernatural power hooked up with you, like the rocket engine on the X-15! Once you were on the other side, it was smooth sailing! The joy of giving and trusting God with your life and your money became a wonderful reality.

Go Through the Gate!

As I taught this to my own congregation, I could imagine them saying to themselves, "Oh, now I get it! This is a tithing sermon! Pastor Bob just wants a big offering. That's all the church wants —money, money, money! That's what he wants." Actually, if all the pastor wanted was your money, it wouldn't be long before he wouldn't be pastor anymore!

The truth of the matter is, no man commands us to tithe; God commands us. Therefore, I don't have to back this up; He does! If you think I am the power behind these Scriptures, you had better not attack Jericho! I stand in the place of Joshua as I write this book. I can only put you in remembrance of what God has said and encourage you to trust His Word.

Loretta and I are living proof that tithing and giving to the Lord makes the difference in lives financially. We have also seen many other believers enter into the land of abundance through this same gateway. Unfortunately, there are many other believers who still want to camp out in the wilderness of just enough.

Even when Israel was in disobedience in the wilderness, God still met their daily needs. He always will, because He's our Father. People often say, "But I thought if we don't tithe, there's a curse." They are referring to Malachi 3:9 where God is telling Israel the reason they are in such trouble is because they have not been tithing. Literally, He says they have been robbing from Him by not tithing.

There is a curse, but the curse applies to the promised land of more than enough, not the wilderness of just enough.

The curse is, we will not enter into the greater blessings of God, into the land of abundance, if we do not step out in faith and obey God's Word by tithing. We stop ourselves by our own disobedience and trap ourselves in the wilderness, living hand to mouth day after day.

If we decide to live in the wilderness, God is still going to meet our daily needs. He is still going to give us our daily provision. He is our God and He cannot forget us. We are His children. As David wrote, "I've never seen the righteous forsaken or His seed begging bread" (Psalm 37:25, author's paraphrase). He promised He would meet our needs, but He wants to provide more than just our needs. He wants to meet the desires of our heart, also.

How long will you camp at the Jordan River? Are you content to settle for less and not enter into the land of abundance? Some of your dreams may never be realized if you do not go through the gates of Jericho! I'm challenging you to get in with God's plan. Watch Him tear down the wall of fear and slay your excuses with His Word. Then give Him the firstfruits of all your labor and watch His abundance begin to flood your life!

2

Our Exceeding Great Reward

If the firstfruits or tithe belong to the Lord, why doesn't He just keep it in the first place? Why does He bless us and ask us to give a tenth back to Him? Because the Lord says to *honor Him* with the firstfruits of all our increase (Proverbs 3:9), and there is no *show of honor* if we don't give to Him.

If the Lord just kept ten percent of our income, there would be no honor for Him to receive. He loves to see us succeed and prosper, but He loves it even more when, of our own free will, we give back to Him.

To the world, money is everything. Money not only buys us the necessities and luxuries of life, but it also gives us an image and status. To the world, how we spend our money tells others what kind of person we are and what is most important to us.

Because unbelievers respect money so much, when we give portions of our money to the Lord, it is a high honor by worldly standards. We are literally giving our life to the Lord when we give Him our money. Ironically, this is true scripturally. The Bible says in Matthew 6:21, "For where your treasure is, there will your heart be also." Even the world knows if we really love and trust God, we will take joy in giving to Him.

Giving our tithes and offerings to the Lord honors Him before the world.

Abram Had an Attitude

One of the greatest (and first) examples of a believer who honored God with the tithe was Abram (whom God later renamed "Abraham" — Genesis 17:5). He saw incredible prosperity and success at every turn because He gave the firstfruits of all he had to God. His attitude toward prosperity was everything he had came from God, and it was his joy to give back to Him. Let's look at the account of the first tithe given to God, which is found in Genesis 14.

And Melchizedek king of Salem brought forth bread and wine: and he was the priest of the most high God.

And he blessed him, and said, Blessed be Abram of the most high God, possessor of heaven and earth:

And blessed be the most high God, which hath delivered thine enemies into thy hand. And he gave him tithes of all.

Genesis 14:18-20

Notice the first time a tithe was given, bread and wine accompanied it. Communion symbolizes our intimate relationship with God through the shed blood and broken body of Jesus Christ. This Scripture tells us that when we give to God, we are worshipping Him and having communion with Him in a very special way.

In this particular situation, by serving communion, Melchizedek was reminding Abram to keep his eyes on the Lord. Abram had just gained great spoils in war and was being tempted to shift his focus to the gifts instead of the Giver. But when he saw the bread and wine, Abram humbly honored the Lord by giving a tenth of all the spoils to Him.

After Abram had honored the Lord with the tithe, the King of Sodom tried to regain some of what he had lost. But long before the King of Sodom could speak to him, Abram had given ten percent to the Lord. There is a principle of prosperity found in Abram's action.

Be quick to give the firstfruits to the Lord before Satan has a chance to try to argue you out of it!

Why is this so important? Not only did Satan try to keep Abram from totally trusting in and honoring the Lord, but in the next chapter of Genesis, we find out Abram was attacked with fear over the entire matter.

After these things the word of the Lord came unto Abram in a vision, saying, Fear not, Abram: I am thy shield, and thy exceeding great reward.

Genesis 15:1

The Lord was gracious to appear to Abram, because just like many of us after he had given the tithe, he went home and panicked, "Good grief! What have I done?"

Have you ever been in a meeting where the Spirit of God began to move through the offering? You thought, "God is speaking to me and I'm going to give today." When you arrived home you wondered if you just sent your last few dollars into oblivion. You even considered calling the bank to stop payment on your check as fear and doubt grabbed your heart and mind. You're in good company. Abram felt the same.

This is very important for you to remember: After the wall of your fears has fallen flat, you will still have to defeat other fears from time to time, even after abundance begins to flow. *If you are not careful, the abundance you experience and then become accustomed to can become your hedge of protection.*

You will be tempted to think, "What if something serious happens to my family? What if some unexpected catastrophe occurs? I need to have something to fall back on, and the money for the tithe could be just what I will need sometime down the road." Your attitude of gratitude is being challenged by fear, worry, and fruitless speculation.

Because of these concerns, the first thing God said to Abram after he tithed was, "Fear not." He assured him He would be his shield. Your finances aren't going to be your shield — God himself will be your shield. If something unexpected comes up, the Lord will be there to deliver you. Don't look to that little bit of money you gave to God. Look to God!

A "Quickly Increasing Money Supply!"

The next thing the Lord tells Abram in Genesis 15:1 is that He is his "exceeding great reward." Usually, it takes several English words to translate one Hebrew word, but "exceeding great reward" is actually a translation of three Hebrew words. It is significant that it took three words to describe what God wanted to say to Abram.

The Hebrew word for "exceeding" is the word *mᵉʼôd*, which means "speedy, fast or quick." The Hebrew word for "great" is *rabah*, which means "increasing." And the Hebrew word for "reward" literally means "salary, wages, or money supply." What did God say to Abram?

I will be your shield and your quickly increasing money supply!

God is simply saying, "I know you gave away a great amount of money, but I will be your reward. Quit looking to yourself or your money for security. Stop putting your faith in what you have in the bank, your own efforts, how many hours you can work, how young you are, or what you've set aside in savings. Those things are fine, but don't put your *trust* in them! Put your trust in Me! I will be your shield and your rapidly increasing supply of finances forever."

Aren't you glad you are not hooked up to this world's economy, but to God's riches in glory? Your next practical question is probably, "But what if I get too old to work?" Abram got old and had the same concern, so God spoke to him about it.

> **And when Abram was ninety years old and nine, the Lord appeared to Abram, and said unto him, I am the Almighty God; walk before me, and be thou perfect.**
>
> **Genesis 17:1**

When God said to Abram, "I am the Almighty God," He wasn't just announcing Himself. This phrase in the Hebrew is "El Shaddai," which literally means, "the all-sufficient one." God doesn't get old and feeble when we do, and He's still the supplier of all our needs when we are ninety years old. He is just as faithful to provide for us in old age as He is during our younger years.

God tells Abram to walk before Him, to keep his eyes on Him, and to be perfect. This just means to grow more and more mature, which is what happens when we find fulfillment in Him, trusting in His Word and obeying. He said, "Abram, just follow My Word. I'll see to it these blessings just keep coming upon you as you are obedient to do what I say."

Tithing in the New Testament

A New Testament analogy for the tithe of Abram to Melchizedek is found in Hebrews, chapter 7.

> **For this Melchisedec, king of Salem, priest of the most high God, who met Abraham returning from the slaughter of the kings, and blessed him;**
>
> **To whom also Abraham gave a tenth part of all; first being by interpretation King of righteousness, and after that also King of Salem, which is, King of peace;**
>
> **Without father, without mother, without descent, having neither beginning of days, nor end of life; but made like unto the Son of God; abideth a priest continually.**
>
> **Hebrews 7:1-3**

Melchizedek represents the Lord Jesus Christ because he is both a king and a priest. There was never a king-priest until Jesus Christ. Although David was a king who acted as a priest, he was only of the kingly tribe. But Melchizedek is said to be a king *and* a priest.

Some have taught that Melchizedek *was* the pre-incarnate Christ, but he was not. He was merely a type and shadow of Him. The Greek literally says, "Having no *recorded* father, no *recorded* mother, and no *recorded* birth or death." (See Hebrews 7:3 AMP.) It doesn't mean Melchizedek didn't have a father or a mother and was an immortal being. It simply means the Bible doesn't say who his father and mother were.

Why is this important? Under the Mosaic law, you had to prove you were of the tribe of Levi to be a priest. But Melchizedek predated the law by some 490 years, appeared suddenly for three verses in Genesis chapter 14 and then was gone. Still, he is a *type* of the Lord Jesus Christ, who had no beginning of days nor end of life, and he was a *man*. The point of this Scripture is even from the beginning, *tithes go to people who represent Jesus Christ.*

Verse three says Melchizedek was "made *like unto* the son of God," but he was not the Son of God, who abides a priest continually. This is Jesus, who is our High Priest forever. Furthermore, when Jesus appeared in the form of a man in the Old Testament, He was always referred to as, "the angel of the Lord." Verse 4 refers to Melchizedek as a man.

> Now consider how great this man [Melchizedek] was, unto whom even the patriarch Abraham gave the tenth of the spoils.
>
> And verily they that are of the sons of Levi, who receive the office of the priesthood, have a commandment to take tithes of the people according to the law, that is, of their brethren, though they come out of the loins of Abraham:
>
> But he whose descent is not counted from them [Melchizedek] received tithes of Abraham, and blessed him that had the promises.

And without all contradiction the less is blessed of the better.

And here men that die receive tithes; but there he receiveth them, of whom it is witnessed that he liveth.

Hebrews 7:4-8

In these verses, the Holy Spirit pulls us into the present day. Now on the earth, men who die receive tithes, but Jesus is the One Whom we honor when we give. Melchizedek is a type of Jesus, Who receives our tithes and offerings. From the time tithes were first instituted in the Word of God, they were given to men who represented the Lord Jesus Christ.

In the same way Melchizedek represented the Lord Jesus, and the temple he ruled over was a type of heaven itself, the pastor represents Jesus and the local church represents His kingdom.

When tithes and offerings are given into the local church, that money will be used to win souls to the Lord and to do the work of the ministry. This is the greatest honor and pleasure to the Lord. But what, in reality, does the Lord Jesus Christ receive from us when we give to Him?

Men Receive Your Money, Jesus Receives Your Attitude

Hebrews 7:8 tells us men receive our tithes and offerings, but the Lord receives our attitude behind them. Have you ever noticed how so many Scriptures on giving always emphasize our attitude? *Honor* the Lord with the firstfruits of your increase. Men who die receive the firstfruits; the Lord receives the honor.

Every man according as he purposeth in his heart, so let him give; not grudgingly, or of necessity: for God loveth a cheerful giver.

Second Corinthians 9:7

39

What happens when we give in faith? Men receive the money, but God receives the faith. What happens when we give in love? Men receive the money, God receives the love. What happens if we give grudgingly or of necessity? Men receive the money, God gets nothing — and we receive nothing back in return. What God uses is the attitude behind the giving.

When we give our finances we give our faith, our love, and our honor to God. Men receive the finances, but God receives our faith, love, and honor. With all these things, God multiplies blessings back to us and brings us out of the land of just enough into the land of abundance.

I hope you are beginning to see how everything in prosperity begins and ends with the Lord Himself. He instructs us to give to Him in faith, and when we choose to obey His Word, He gives us the courage to face all our fears and excuses. Through His supernatural strength, we then overcome those fears and excuses and step out in faith to obey His Word. We then give our tithes and offerings to men who die, but our faith, love, and honor to God.

Because you have come to worship Him with your tithes and offerings, surrendering your life to Him as you give, He becomes more real in your daily life. You can feel His presence at every turn, and His Spirit will give you wisdom to meet every challenge — financial and otherwise. He has truly become your "exceeding great reward."

3
Command Your Family

One of the reasons Abraham is considered a great man of faith is because he was the first person the Bible records as giving the tithe to the Lord. But if we dig a little deeper into his life, it is interesting to discover what the Lord said about Abraham.

> **For I know him, that he will command his children and his household after him, and they shall keep the way of the Lord, to do justice and judgment; that the Lord may bring upon Abraham that which he hath spoken of him.**
>
> **Genesis 18:19**

God chose Abraham to be the father of Israel for a very specific reason: Abraham would command his family. What God saw in Abraham was the husband and father who would be the leader of his family. He would see to it that his wife, children, and even his grandchildren were taught the Word of God and would learn to walk in the ways of the Lord.

Passing the Torch

It is important for a man to be a friend to his wife and children, but the most important thing is to be a leader. The family needs someone who will not only *tell* them what should be done and what is right, but who will set the example by *doing* it. The man should be an example in every area of the Word of God — including finances.

Abraham taught his son Isaac and Isaac taught his son Jacob about God's principles of prosperity. By implication, we know Abraham taught Isaac the principle of the tithe. In Genesis 26:1-14, there is an account of how Isaac obeyed the Lord and sowed in famine. He received a hundred-fold return on what he sowed.

There is even stronger evidence that Abraham and Isaac taught Jacob the principle of the tithe in chapter 28 of Genesis. Here Jacob has a personal encounter with the Lord and must make the decision whether to serve Him or not. Until now, he has been following the Lord as his grandfather and father instructed him, but he has never made that decision for himself.

Part of passing the torch of the gospel to the next generation is giving our children the understanding they must know God themselves. They cannot depend upon us for their salvation, direction in life, knowledge, or wisdom. There comes a time in each person's life when they have to decide to accept the Lord, serve Him, and grow up in Him for themselves.

We're not a Christian because our parents were Christians. Blessings don't come to us just because our parents are believers and are praying for us. The Bible can be taught to us, but eventually we have to have a personal encounter with the Lord Jesus Christ and choose to believe God's Word for ourself.

Jacob's Encounter

And Jacob went out from Beer-sheba, and went toward Haran.

And he lighted upon a certain place, and tarried there all night, because the sun was set; and he took of the stones of that place, and put them for his pillows, and lay down in that place to sleep.

And he dreamed, and behold a ladder set up on the earth, and the top of it reached to heaven: and behold the angels of God ascending and descending on it.

And, behold, the Lord stood above it, and said, I am the Lord God of Abraham thy father, and the God of

Isaac: the land whereon thou liest, to thee will I give it, and to thy seed;

And thy seed shall be as the dust of the earth, and thou shalt spread abroad to the west, and to the east, and to the north, and to the south: and in thee and in thy seed shall all the families of the earth be blessed.

And, behold, I am with thee, and will keep thee in all places whither thou goest, and will bring thee again into this land; for I will not leave thee, until I have done that which I have spoken to thee of.

And Jacob awaked out of his sleep, and he said, Surely the Lord is in this place; and I knew it not.

And he was afraid, and said, How dreadful is this place! this is none other but the house of God, and this is the gate of heaven.

And Jacob rose up early in the morning, and took the stone that he had put for his pillows, and set it up for a pillar, and poured oil upon the top of it.

And he called the name of that place Beth-el: but the name of that city was called Luz at the first.

And Jacob vowed a vow, saying, If God will be with me, and will keep me in this way that I go, and will give me bread to eat, and raiment to put on,

So that I come again to my father's house in peace; then shall the Lord be my God:

And this stone, which I have set for a pillar, shall be God's house: and of all that thou shalt give me I will surely give the tenth unto thee.
Genesis 28:10-22

Jacob also came to a gateway of decision in his life. In his dream, the angels ascending and descending the ladder were the messengers of God who would bring His blessings to Jacob. Among those were the financial blessings that would come as a result of obedience to tithe and give offerings unto the Lord. Jacob's ladder is a beautiful picture of Malachi 3:10, that our tithe opens the windows of heaven enabling God to pour His prosperity into our lives.

Jacob received the same promises God had made to his grandfather, Abraham, and his father, Isaac. When he awoke, he called the place Bethel, which means "the house of the Lord." He made a dedication to give a tenth of everything He was blessed with to God.

After that dream, the Lord did bless Jacob. God told Jacob in the dream he would be leaving His country for a while, but one day he would come back and inherit it. We see the fulfillment of that promise in Genesis 32:10, when Jacob says, "I am not worthy of the least of all the mercies, and of all the truth, which thou hast shewed unto thy servant; for with my staff I passed over this Jordan; and now I am become two bands."

Literally, Jacob is saying he left with nothing but a staff in his hand, but because of the Lord's blessing, he is returning with two bands. "Bands" means a great number of people, such as would be in an army. He now has two wives, children, servants, cattle, gold, silver, and fine clothing, among other things.

Looking at Jacob's story, we can see how tithing doesn't begin when great finances come in. Tithing begins with a decision: "From now on, whatever money comes in, I'm going to give a tenth of it to God." When Jacob settled the issue of tithing, he didn't have anything. He began by taking stones and making an altar unto the Lord, because the Lord had appeared to him and revealed His greatness. Then, as an act of worship and gratitude, he pledged to give back a tenth of all the Lord gave him.

We are a part in the same spiritual heritage as Abraham, Isaac, and Jacob. The same promises given to them have been given to us. But like Jacob, we need to have a personal encounter with the Lord Jesus concerning our finances. We need to make up our mind from now on He is always going to receive ten percent right off the top; the firstfruits belong to Him.

Before Jacob came back a wealthy, successful man, he went through tremendous trials. God saw him through each one, and when he returned he returned with a thankful heart, never losing his love for the Lord. Possessions, wives, children, servants, cattle, and all those things didn't turn his eyes away from the Lord, his first priority.

Solomon's Encounter

My son, forget not my law; but let thine heart keep my commandments:

Honour the Lord with thy substance, and with the firstfruits of all thine increase:

So shall thy barns be filled with plenty, and thy presses shall burst out with new wine.

My son, despise not the chastening of the Lord; neither be weary of his correction:

For whom the Lord loveth he correcteth; even as a father the son in whom he delighteth.

My son, let not them depart from thine eyes: keep sound wisdom and discretion.

Proverbs 3:1,9-10,11-12,21

Like the rest of the book of Proverbs, these verses contain wisdom from Solomon. David set an example for his son Solomon by living God's principles before him, just as Abraham taught Isaac and Isaac taught Jacob. But there came a day when the Lord personally appeared to Solomon. He had learned all the things David had taught him, but Solomon had to have a personal encounter with the Lord and make the decision to serve Him.

In Gibeon the Lord appeared to Solomon in a dream by night: and God said, Ask what I shall give thee.

And Solomon said, Thou hast shewed unto thy servant David my father great mercy, according as he walked before thee in truth, and in righteousness, and in uprightness of heart with thee; and thou hast kept

for him this great kindness, that thou hast given him a son to sit on his throne, as it is this day.

And now, Oh Lord my God, thou hast made thy servant king instead of David my father: and I am but a little child: I know not how to go out or come in.

And thy servant is in the midst of thy people which thou hast chosen, a great people, that cannot be numbered nor counted for multitude.

Give therefore thy servant an understanding heart to judge thy people, that I may discern between good and bad: for who is able to judge this thy so great a people?

First Kings 3:5-9

The Lord appeared to Solomon and told him he could have anything he wanted. Most people would have probably rubbed their hands together and said, "Oh, boy! I've been dreaming about this for a long time. Lord, I want so much wealth that nobody in the world will even come near it. I want the best looking chariots in the world. I want my castle to be the biggest in the land. I want a walk-in closet that will take two days to walk from one end to the other. I want to have the most gorgeous garments in all the kingdom. And besides that, Lord, I want my friends to be the most powerful and affluent people in the world. Oh, and by the way Lord, if anybody ever attacks me, I want an army that will crush them in a day's time."

But what did Solomon ask for? Wisdom. In his first personal encounter with God, he simply asked for wisdom. All the training and teaching he received from his father and mother were good, but it was time for him to make a personal dedication to the Lord, to put Him first in all things just as his parents had done.

God was so pleased with Solomon's answer, He not only granted him a "wise and understanding heart," but everything he *didn't* ask for — riches, honor, and victory over his enemies. (See First Kings 3:10-13) When Solomon heard that, he went to the temple and sacrificed both burnt offerings and peace offerings to the Lord in gratitude and worship. He wrote:

Happy is the man that findeth wisdom, and the man that getteth understanding.

For the merchandise of it is better than the merchandise of silver, and the gain thereof than fine gold.

She is more precious than rubies: and all the things thou canst desire are not to be compared unto her.

Length of days is in her right hand; and in her left hand riches and honour.

Proverbs 3:13-16

The Hebrew word translated "merchandise" means profit. The profit of wisdom is better than that of silver or gold. She — wisdom — is more precious than rubies, and nothing can be compared to her. In fact, everything Solomon did *not* ask for, which God gave him *anyway*, is a result of wisdom — long life, riches, and honor.

Head of the Home

We have seen how *Abraham* was confronted by Melchizedek and made the decision to tithe to the Lord. We have seen how *Jacob* was met by the Lord, Who stood at the top of the ladder while he was at the bottom of the ladder, and between him and the Lord were angels ascending and descending up to heaven and back down to earth.

We have seen how the Lord approached *Solomon,* asking him what he wanted, and because Solomon asked for wisdom to judge God's people, God also gave him riches, honor, and long life. In a previous chapter, we saw that before the children of Israel could conquer Jericho, the men, or the *heads of the households,* had to be circumcised. What is the significance of all these examples?

Each time the Lord brought a commandment about tithing and honoring Him first, He approached the head of the household; He came to the man.

Today there is a great drought across this nation and around the world of men who will stand up and set the example for their family. David passed along wisdom about this to Solomon, who would be the head of his home. Solomon wrote, "Before you marry and have a family, make the decision to honor the Lord with the firstfruits of all your increase. Then your barns will be filled with plenty and your presses will burst with new wine" (author's paraphrase). David was not telling Solomon anything he hadn't already demonstrated in his own life.

Often we see fathers who will teach their children the right way, but they don't set the example themselves. Remember the old saying, "Do as I say not as I do"? The greatest thing a husband and father can do in the family is to *show* his wife and children the right way. By *doing* the right thing, the men rise up and become the leaders God wants them to be.

Jacob hadn't even met his wife when the Lord appeared to him. God came to Jacob and said, "Before you even get started, I want you to know as I was to Abram I am your shield and your exceeding great reward. I stand at the top of the ladder and between you and Me, Jacob, there are angels ascending to My throne to bring your petitions, then descending from My throne to bring the supply back to you" (author's paraphrase).

Suddenly, Jacob understood what the Lord was saying. Great things were about to come to him. Because of this he made the decision to surrender his entire life to the Lord and built an altar saying, "Lord, I dedicate myself to you. From now on, whatever you bless me with, even as my grandfather Abraham and my father Isaac tithed to You, I will tithe to You. You will be my shield and my exceeding great reward" (author's paraphrase).

Because of that decision, when Jacob returned years later with great riches, he had a heart of gratitude and worship, saying, "Lord you did all of this. All I did was go out with a staff in my hand, but I have come back with wives, children, servants, and many possessions. I return with all these things, and all the praise goes to You, Lord" (author's paraphrase).

The Bible sets down a principle declaring husbands to be responsible for their families. In the Old Testament, God dealt severely with whole families because of the sins of the father. An example of this was Achan, who disobeyed the command of the Lord and stole some of the spoils of Jericho, keeping them for himself. He buried them in his tent, so no one knew except the Lord, and the Lord told Joshua.

As a result of his disobedience, a curse came on Achan's family and they were all killed. Just as a husband stands in the place to bless his family, he also stands in the place to bring poverty to his family. *A husband and father is the gateway into the home.*

It is time for each man in the Church to make their house the house of God. It is time for them to build an altar in their house and say, "As for me and my house, we will serve the Lord."

It is time for men to quit looking to their job as their source of supply or their paycheck as their financial security. The Lord is the supplier of their lives. The job is merely a channel for God to send blessings into the family. With trust in the Lord, God can open other channels of blessing from unknown sources. The ladder had many angels coming from God, not one or two. There is no force on this earth that can stop the angels from bringing the blessings of God into the home of a man who is walking in obedience to God's Word by giving tithes and offerings.

Of course, the question immediately arises from some of the women, "But I don't have a husband. He left me and the kids; he doesn't have a job; and he doesn't send me any money or help in any way. What happens in my case?"

God acknowledges single-parent women as the designated leader of their family, and the same blessings that would come to Jacob will come to them.

Although there is no husband, God still wants to supply each need. The One Who stands at the top of the ladder is not the ex-husband! The One Who stands at the top of the ladder is Jesus Christ. And walking up and down that ladder are not alimony and child support checks, but mighty angels who supply through God's abundance, not the ex-husband's lack.

The same thing happened to a woman in the Old Testament. In Genesis, chapter 21, Hagar was forced to leave Abraham's house with their son Ishmael. God said she had to go; Abraham's house would not be blessed as long as she and Ishmael were there.

When Hagar left the house, Abraham gave her bread and a wineskin filled with water. That was her alimony check, and it ran out about ten miles down the road. At that point, she said, "Lord, I'm just going to sit down here and die." She took her son and laid him under a shrub, then moved away so she wouldn't see him die.

At this point the Lord appeared to her, assured her He had a plan for her life as well as for her son, and then showed her a well. Men may give a bottle of water, but Jesus wants to give a well which will not run dry! If there is no man around, Jesus becomes the husband.

Make Your Home Bethel

No matter who you are or what your circumstances may be, it is time to make your home Bethel, the house of the Lord. Establish your heart that from now on, whatever the Lord blesses you with, a tenth belongs to Him. Don't do it only for your sake, but for your family's sake as well. Set the Word of God before your children not only by teaching, but by example. Show them God's Word works!

Say to yourself, "It's time my family quit living in the land of just enough, barely getting along from paycheck to paycheck. I'm dedicating my finances to the Lord by tithing and giving with worship and gratitude. We are going to shout with joy and faith at the wall of fear and excuses, watch the wall come crashing down, and enter the land of abundance!"

The same God who went with Jacob is the same God who will go with you. I'm not telling you it will be smooth sailing and everything will be wonderful. I'm simply saying God's power is going to back His Word as you obey Him in giving Him the firstfruits. No matter how Satan tries to stop you, God is going to reverse it and turn everything around for your blessing.

You are going to see people try to come against you and keep you from prospering, but God is going to laugh and say, "Watch what I'm going to do." He will turn Satan's plans of poverty around, and you'll find yourself increasing your tithe instead of decreasing it.

You may begin with a staff in your hand, but eventually you're going to come in with two hosts, so blessed by God you cannot understand it! All this will come to pass because you decided to serve Him and put Him first in every area of your life, including your finances.

See that ladder in front of you? You are standing on the earth, and Jesus is standing at the top. See those mighty angels ascending and descending? One angel can defeat an army, and you have multitudes of them going up with your prayers and petitions and coming back down with God's answers and abundance!

Because you have commanded your family in the ways of the Lord, all the blessings of Abraham are yours!

4

How An Offering Comes to Life

Unless the Holy Spirit anoints and energizes whatever we do, whether it is praying for the sick or giving an offering, that work is dead. How do we know this? Throughout the Word of God, it is the Holy Spirit who brings things or people to life. If the Holy Spirit is not present, there is no life.

The first time we see the Holy Spirit bring something to life is in Genesis, chapter 1. The Scripture tells us how the earth had become without form, void (lifeless), and darkness covered the face of the deep. But then the Holy Spirit began to "move" upon the face of the waters.

The Hebrew word for "move" means to brood or incubate. Just as a mother hen sits upon her eggs to bring her baby chicks to life, the Holy Spirit "moved" upon the earth. Heavenly warmth came to this earth and life began to come forth. God placed living creatures upon it and filled the waters with fish.

The sixth day God created man. He created man out of the dust of the ground, but man was still lifeless until God's life was breathed into his body. The same principle — that all life comes from God's Spirit — is true in our lives. Until we meet the Lord Jesus Christ and receive Him as Lord and Savior, we are spiritually dead creatures, lost and dead in trespasses and sin, separated from God. We might have natural life, but we don't have spiritual life. Thus, the Holy Spirit "moves" over us, drawing us to Jesus.

One day we decide to take that step of faith and choose to believe in Jesus as our Savior and Lord. As we believe in Jesus, the Holy Spirit breathes eternal life into us. Our dead spirit becomes alive, and we enter into a whole new realm. When the Holy Spirit breathes new life into us, it is not a natural or momentary life, but an *eternal* life. Nothing has eternal value if it is not brought to life by God's Spirit — including tithes and offerings.

The Power in a Seed

We want our tithes and offerings to have eternal value, so how do we bring the life of the Holy Spirit into our giving? Throughout the Word of God, giving is compared to sowing seed. For example, in Second Corinthians 9:6 it says, "He which soweth sparingly shall reap also sparingly; and he which soweth bountifully shall reap also bountifully."

This verse is simply saying, when we withhold from giving, it will lead to poverty, but when we give generously, it will lead to great prosperity. God wants us to know, when we're generous in His kingdom, the Holy Spirit energizes our tithes and offerings and brings a generous return. Just as one seed planted in good soil grows into a larger plant and produces many seeds, our giving brings multiplied prosperity to us.

Money has the ability to reproduce, both naturally and supernaturally. We can invest money wisely today and get back more money tomorrow by natural means. Money has *seed potential*. But only when energized by the Holy Spirit does it have a supernatural potential and eternal value. No where in this earth can we plant and have a miraculous return except in the kingdom of God.

The same eternal life that was imparted to us at the new birth can be imparted into our offering. You may ask, "Eternal life into finances?" Yes! The financial seed we plant into the gospel not only comes up through our lifetime, but keeps producing into the next generation and eternally in heaven.

Many people over the years have given into ministries such as Billy Graham's. Thousands of people have been saved through his ministry, and they have in turn led others to the Lord. Therefore, the people who gave their finances to support Billy Graham's ministry are still seeing a return on their investment, even if they have gone on to be with the Lord!

Offerings have the ability to keep on working long after we are gone, just like natural seeds planted in the past. When we plant a seed from a pear, that seed eventually grows into a pear tree. Then year after year, that pear tree will produce pears and the seeds from those pears will produce more pear trees and more pears.

From planting one little seed, a tremendous amount of fruit is produced over many years. In the same way, the finances we sow into God's kingdom today will produce much fruit.

The Power in a Ritual

Because we want our tithes and offerings to please the Lord and become energized by the Holy Spirit, it becomes very important that we know *how* to give to the Lord. In the Word of God there are rituals attached to many things we do, and giving into God's kingdom is one example.

"Ritual" related to everything in the Old Testament. There was more ritual in the Old Testament than there is in the New Testament, because the rituals taught of God's plan of redemption and the coming Messiah. In the New Testament, because Jesus has already come to fulfill the plan of redemption, there are only three rituals given: anointing with oil, water baptism, and communion.

Never let any of these rituals lose their meaning! Many believers come from denominations which were filled with dead, meaningless rituals, and that was the extent of their Christian experience — dead works. But ritual is not spawned out of ritual; ritual is spawned out of *reality*.

Somewhere in the past, that denomination had a move of God. Rituals were formed from the revelation of God's Word at that time. As time passed, the reality of that fresh revelation faded, but the ritual remained. The people continue to come to church and perform the ritual, but they don't know what it means. The revelation has been lost.

Those of us who were raised in Sunday school can remember how often the teacher would have us recite the Lord's prayer. Our mind would focus on everything except the Lord's prayer, yet we would recite it perfectly from memory. We said it so often that today we can still say it flawlessly and never think about what we are saying.

The same thing often happens when we pray over a meal or when we pray for somebody to be healed. We pray a prayer we have prayed a hundred times. There's nothing wrong with praying the same prayer if we don't lose the meaning of it. *We must think about what we're saying!*

When we partake of communion, I exhort the people to remember what they are doing. They are not just eating a cracker and drinking a little juice. When we forget the reason for communion, we will become weak, sick, and die early by not honoring the cup and the bread just as the believers did in First Corinthians 11:30. On the other hand, when we show honor and acknowledge the significance of communion, great blessings can come into our life. There is no blessing in ritual, but there is tremendous blessing in the *meaning* of the ritual.

When we anoint people with oil, it is not the oil that heals, but "the prayer of faith shall save the sick, and the

Lord shall raise him up" (James 5:15). Without understanding and faith behind it, anointing with oil means nothing and the prayer becomes a lifeless exercise, bringing no results.

The same principle applies to water baptism. Unless we understand water baptism, it is a meaningless ritual. Those who know the power of water baptism have come out of the water speaking with tongues, experiencing divine healing, or revelation from God. It wasn't the ritual that brought about speaking in tongues or healing, it was understanding the incredible meaning of what they were doing — the old man died with Jesus and the new man was being raised with Him in resurrection power!

Ritual was never designed by God to be something we do without remembering the meaning. God's rituals are full of meaning and wonderful teachings. The rituals of the Old Testament can apply to our life as well. We are going to study a ritual pertaining to the giving of our finances.

A Ritual for Giving

In Deuteronomy 26, God gave a ritual to Israel concerning giving.

The purpose of this ritual was to properly present the firstfruits to God. When He commanded Israel to do it, they had not entered into the promised land yet. He said, "Before you enter the promised land, I'm going to give you instructions on how to give. I don't want you to focus on the ritual itself, but understand the meaning behind it" (author's paraphrase).

> **And it shall be, when thou art come in unto the land which the Lord thy God giveth thee for an inheritance, and possessest it, and dwellest therein;**
>
> **That thou shalt take of the first of all the fruit of the earth, which thou shalt bring of thy land that the Lord thy God giveth thee, and shalt put it in a basket, and**

shalt go unto the place which the Lord thy God shall choose to place his name there.

And thou shalt go unto the priest that shall be in those days, and say unto him, I profess this day unto the Lord thy God, that I am come unto the country which the Lord sware unto our fathers for to give us.

And the priest shall take the basket out of thine hand, and set it down before the altar of the Lord thy God.

Deuteronomy 26:1-4

We can break this ritual down into four areas:

1. *Now, we have entered the land.* In the first verse, God talked about the reality of entering and possessing the land. Once we have broken through our walls of fears, we are no longer in the wilderness of "just enough." We have now entered our land of Abundance. There needs to come into our lives a new way of thinking. Changing positions must be followed with a change of attitude. There had to be as dramatic of a mental change from the wilderness to Canaan as there had been from Egypt to the desert.

The act of the initial tithe puts us across Jordan. The wall of fear has fallen flat, and we are now in the land. We may look around and say, "Well, it doesn't feel different, and it doesn't look different." But it is different. The battles are not over, but *we are in the land.* Our attitude toward giving will be completely different when our attitude about our surroundings change. The days of struggling with just enough are coming to an end. Our days of plenty and abundance are just beginning.

There are two outward acts that accompany the revelation of knowing we have entered the land. These are brought out in verses 3 and 4.

First, Israel was to bring their offering before the priest, who was God's representative. When Abraham brought the tithe, he presented it to the Lord through the priest named Melchizedek.

We have already seen from the Word of God that priests are human beings and that Melchizedek was a human being. We bring our tithes and offerings into the local church and present them to our pastor.

Often we use the human weaknesses of the minister as an excuse to withhold our tithes and offerings. We see them make mistakes, are offended, and then refuse to give. We forget we are not really giving to them, but to God. They are standing in their God-given position.

Secondly, we build our altar. We don't just come and give to the church, but we bring our gift to an altar *we* have prepared, which is our dedication to the Lord. In Psalms and other passages it's called a *vow*, which is simply a commitment to the Lord.

The altar of dedication and our vow to the Lord becomes a point of stability in our lives. Why do we come to church week after week? Why is it important that we not neglect "the assembling of ourselves together" (Hebrews 10:25)? Meeting with other believers to worship the Lord and to be taught His Word brings us back to fundamentals, moves our priorities in line, and gives us a healthy, balanced perspective.

If we have failed to evaluate ourselves according to God's Word during our busy week, coming to the altar of dedication in church will put us in remembrance. We can look back on our week and say, "Lord, I made so many mistakes and overlooked opportunities to witness for you. I didn't do the best job possible on my family. Please forgive me."

In the Old Testament, it was the giving of their offerings to the Lord that constituted Israel's altar of commitment. When they took their tithes and offerings and gave them to the Lord in worship and gratitude, it brought them back to reality and put them in remembrance of what was really important.

For us in the New Testament, it says, "Now concerning the collection for the saints, as I have given order to the churches of Galatia, even so do ye. Upon the first day of the week let every one of you lay by him in store, as God hath prospered him" (First Corinthians 16:1,2). Giving is a great stabilizer for us. Because our finances represent our lives, giving to the Lord is an intimate expression of surrendering ourselves again to the Lord and putting Him first in all things.

During praise and worship, special music, and the preaching and teaching of God's Word, we are receiving and learning. But, during the offering we dramatically give ourselves to God. God sees it as holy, and it is a point of consecration for all believers.

To sum up this first point, we have entered the land. We live in the revelation that we *are* prosperous in Christ, bringing our firstfruits to God's representative at the altar of dedication, a ritual that is filled with meaning. As we bring our finances to our human priest, we are surrendering ourselves to our High Priest, the Lord Jesus Christ. This brings stability and joy to our lives.

> **And thou shalt speak and say before the Lord thy God, A Syrian ready to perish was my father, and he went down into Egypt, and sojourned there with a few, and became there a nation, great, mighty, and populous:**
>
> **And the Egyptians evil entreated us, and afflicted us, and laid upon us hard bondage:**
>
> **And when we cried unto the Lord God of our fathers, the Lord heard our voice, and looked on our affliction, and our labour, and our oppression:**
>
> **And the Lord brought us forth out of Egypt with a mighty hand, and with an outstretched arm, and with great terribleness, and with signs, and with wonders:**
>
> **Deuteronomy 26:5-8**

2. The offering represents the grace of God in our time. We can see this in the above verses as the Jews describe what the Lord has done for them over the years.

As they present the firstfruits as directed in verses 1 through 4, they are told in verses 5 through 8 to then express their thanksgiving for what the Lord had done for them over the years in miracles, signs and wonders. Verses 6 through 8 give the account of Israel being oppressed in Egypt and then being delivered. The Lord had brought them from the point of being "a Syrian ready to perish" (v. 5) to being a great and mighty nation whom He delivered from oppression through great and mighty wonders. Our tithes and offerings represent the time God has worked in our lives and on our behalf.

Our offering doesn't just represent the past two weeks of work. It represents years of miracles, signs, and wonders!

When young ministers ask me how long it takes me to prepare a sermon, I never know what to say. Because I have been teaching the Bible for so many years, it takes me a lot less time to prepare a sermon now than it did twenty years ago. I could say that it takes me several days — plus the past twenty years — to prepare a sermon today.

Let's say a man has been a carpenter for ten years. By now he can work so fast and skillfully that within days he has a house framed and the roof on it. If someone asks how long it took to frame a house, he might say four days. But if he considers how long he has been a carpenter, his answer would be *ten years* and four days.

The length of time becomes relative because of the amount of time behind it. When we come to church and present our tithes, we might look at our checks and say, "Well, this tithe check represents about two weeks of my life." But according to verses 5-8, the tithe made on our paychecks doesn't only represent two weeks' work, but all the years God has taught us and provided for us as well.

Every time we give an offering, it represents the years God has been working on our behalf, before and after we were born again. Therefore, what we give to Him started a long time ago and it didn't start with us, it started with Him. *He's* the One Who blessed *us*. He's the One Who sought us out. And He's the One Who redeemed us and prospered us so we could give back to Him.

In many Scriptures, especially the Psalms, God continues to say, "Remember the Red Sea; don't forget any of My benefits. Look back and remember how I delivered you out of bondage. Remember how I brought the wall of Jericho down." If we will do this when we give to the Lord, we will say, "This offering began a long time ago, Lord. It doesn't just represent the past few days, but many years of your grace in my life."

And he hath brought us into this place, and hath given us this land, even a land that floweth with milk and honey.

Deuteronomy 26:9

3. *God brings you every blessing you have.* In this verse, God reminds Israel that He's the One Who gave the pillar of fire by night to keep them warm and the cloud by day to shield them from the burning sun in the wilderness. He's the One Who brought them water, quail, and manna in the wilderness, led them through the Jordan River, and made the wall of Jericho fall flat.

When Israel began working *with* God by entering the promised land and taking Jericho, all the blessings of that land had already been prepared by God for them. In the same way, every blessing we enjoy as believers comes from Him.

Nevertheless, how often do we brag about our works? "Wow, did I give a great offering last week!" "I worked so hard to get that promotion, and it finally came!" "What a deal I pulled off today! I knew exactly what to say to that customer!" But who gave us the offering to give, favor with the boss, and the wisdom to speak?

Our obedience is essential to receive the blessings, but we should never forget He is the One Who blesses us in all things. It's not the size of our *offerings* that impresses God, but the size of our *thanksgiving!* Our offering is the seed, but our attitude of thanksgiving and worship is the power in the seed. What causes the seed to become supernatural is when we remember all the good things God has done for us, that every blessing has come from Him.

Our works are not our own personal accomplishments. Everything we do is through the grace of God and with the help of others. Every good thing that comes our way comes from His hand and is often delivered to us through the hands of men. When we give our tithes and offerings humbly to Him with this truth in mind, He is pleased and our gifts will produce for Him and for us.

> **And now, behold, I have brought the firstfruits of the land, which thou, O Lord, hast given me. And thou shalt set it before the Lord thy God, and worship before the Lord thy God.**
>
> **Deuteronomy 26:10**

4. *Worship the Lord with your firstfruits.* God told Israel to *worship* Him with the firstfruits because He did not want the last thing they remembered to be their offering, but God, Who received it. They brought the firstfruits and planted the seed, but the last thing they did was worship the Lord. They turned their attention to Him.

God doesn't want us walking away from the offering remembering how big our offerings were. He wants us to remember how big He is! God is not waiting on us to bless Him. He's waiting to bless us. Giving is simply our act of obedience, which frees Him to give back to us "good measure, pressed down, and shaken together, and running over" (Luke 6:38).

When we are in heaven, the praises are not going to be about our giving. God will not call us out one by one and say, "I remember the day you gave your greatest offering." Throughout eternity, we are going to remember one gift, one tithe, one firstfruits offering which God gave on a cross — Jesus! Whatever we give to God, we give in response to *His offering*. We give because of the shed blood and broken body of Jesus Christ, which brought us salvation and grace in every area of our lives.

In Psalm 116:12 David says, "What shall I render unto the Lord for all of his benefits toward me? I will take the cup of salvation, and call upon the name of the Lord."

Salvation is the first thing David thanked God for. The offering we have in our hands should remind us how God saved us and how He has brought us through every difficult situation. We also remember He *continues* to deliver us today.

David couldn't wait to get to the tabernacle to give his firstfruits to the Lord. Verse 13 tells us he wanted to do it in front of everyone — not to brag on himself, but to publicly give glory to God. He wanted to be there when the whole congregation gave to the Lord, to be a part of that holy and blessed time of worship unto God.

David says in verse 17, "I will offer to thee the sacrifice of thanksgiving, and will call upon the name of the Lord." David offered thanksgiving unto God and called upon the name of the Lord. We shouldn't walk away from the church service remembering the great offering we gave. We need to walk away remembering the great offering God gave us — Jesus.

What is it that brings Holy Ghost power to our giving? What is it that resurrects our seed and gives our tithes and offerings eternal life? Simply our attitude of worship and praise, acknowledging His mercy and grace and His power

64

and deliverance. When we worship God with our tithes and offerings in spirit and in truth, we infuse His life into the seed we plant. From that moment, our seed begins to grow and will produce supernaturally and eternally!

5
Lord of the Earth

As believers, we know Jesus Christ is Lord of the earth. The Bible says in Psalm 50:12, "The world is mine, and the fulness thereof." We also know that we receive our income from Him. He is the One Who provides for us and blesses us. However, not *all* our income is holy. Only the part we separate unto Him is holy. The rest of it is used for natural things throughout the week, such as food, gas for our cars, paying house payments, and all those things that are normal, everyday activities.

Dying to Ourselves in Giving

The part of our income that is holy are the tithes and offerings we give to the Lord. This money becomes separated and consecrated unto Him as the firstfruits of our income. In the Old Testament, we have already seen how Jericho was the firstfruits Israel was to give to the Lord. Everything and everyone in the city but Rahab and her household was to be an offering unto Him.

And the city shall be accursed, even it, and all that are therein, to the Lord: only Rahab the harlot shall live, she and all that are with her in the house, because she hid the messengers that we sent.

And ye, in any wise keep yourselves from the accursed thing, lest ye make yourselves accursed, when ye take of the accursed thing, and make the camp of Israel a curse, and trouble it.

> **But all the silver, and gold, and vessels of brass and iron, are consecrated unto the Lord: they shall come into the treasury of the Lord.**
>
> **Joshua 6:17-19**

In verses 17 and 18, the word "accursed" is mentioned several times. "Accursed" is the Hebrew word *cherem,* it doesn't really mean cursed. In the purest form, it means "to be separated in either a good sense or a bad sense."

A more accurate definition of *cherem* would be "to be separated unto God's own use." Consequently, when we hold onto or tamper with what God has said is His, we are separating ourself from Him, which is a cursed place to be. He is simply saying, "This is separated unto Me, so don't make it part of your life. Give it to Me so I can work with it and bless you through it."

Another definition for *cherem* is "to throw a net over." God was simply saying to Israel, "When you come to the city of Jericho, throw a net over it and give it to Me." Joshua was to instruct the people that Jericho belonged to God. In essence, as they gave that city over to God, it was separated unto Him as the firstfruits, which always belong to the Lord. He said, "Once it is given to Me, it becomes holy" (author's paraphrase).

The word *cherem* is also mentioned in Leviticus 27:28.

> **Notwithstanding no devoted thing, that a man shall devote unto the Lord of all that he hath, both of man and beast, and of the field of his possession, shall be sold or redeemed: every devoted thing is most holy unto the Lord.**

The word "devoted" is the same Hebrew word, *cherem.* The Lord is simply saying that anything we consecrate to Him is most holy. Whether it is money we earned while working at our job or the time and efforts spent in ministry, we look at it as something God is taking to multiply and put to work in His kingdom.

After we give God the firstfruits of our increase, there are still portions left for our personal use. The Lord told Joshua that after Jericho, Ai and all the other cities belonged to them. In the future, there would be more tithes and freewill offerings given to the Lord, but the bulk of the spoils would be distributed among the people for their own use. Jericho was the firstfruits that belonged to the Lord in its entirety.

If we go on in Leviticus 27:29 we find something very interesting.

None devoted, which shall be devoted of men, shall be redeemed; but shall surely be put to death.

In verse 28, God said every devoted or separated thing is most holy unto the Lord. Then in verse 29, He says those things you separate and sanctify for God's use cannot be redeemed or taken back, but must be put to death. From the previous verses, we know He is referring to crops, animals, men — all we possess and all the spoils of war.

This does not mean God was commanding Israel to sacrifice the firstfruits of their families, along with the crops and animals. God only required one human sacrifice, which was Jesus. However, the firstborn in the family *was* an offering to the Lord in another way.

The firstborn son was separated into God's service by entering the priesthood. Later, God consecrated the entire tribe of Levi, which represented the firstborn, to be His priesthood. The other tribes would financially support the tribe of Levi so they could devote themselves to serving God.

By dedicating the first son to God, in a way the parents let him die to them. They had to turn him over to God and release him. He belonged to God, not to them, and he would serve God, not them. In essence, they had to crucify their flesh by giving their first son to the Lord. They did this in the same way they gave the firstfruits of all their increase to God, whether it was money, cattle or wheat.

Unlike the firstborn son, however, the firstfruits of their animals and crops had to physically die. They couldn't go back to the priest later and say, "Hey, I decided I want that lamb back." By then it had been put to death as an offering unto the Lord. Nor could they retrieve their tithe of crops. If they went back a few days later and asked to have their barley returned to them, the priest would probably point to a loaf of bread on his plate. Their barley had been crushed, made into loaves, and baked as food for the priests.

When they gave their firstfruits to God, whether it was their firstborn son, their animals, their money, or their crops, they died to it. This is what made it holy unto the Lord. In the same way, when we give our tithe to the Lord, we are to totally give it and die to it. Let Him do with it as He pleases, and He promises to bless you in return.

A death to selfishness has to take place when we give. It is the same death to selfishness the children of Israel encountered after they took Jericho. The people conquered the city, saw all the gold and silver and treasures, but they placed them in the treasury of the Lord. To Israel, Jericho's riches were dead which made the treasure holy to God.

The Hebrew word for firstfruits is *bikkur*, which means "the first ripe," and the Greek word is *aparache*, which means "beginning." These words refer to the first and the finest. The first and finest apples on the tree were the ones belonging to the Lord. The first and finest animals were given to the Lord. The firstborn (which designated him the finest) son was dedicated and separated unto the work of the Lord.

When the firstfruits was given to the Lord, and the people released it, it was totally in God's hands. *This portion became the guarantee for God and for them that the rest of their* crop, *their herd, or their children would be good.* The firstfruits was given to the Lord in gratitude and worship, not only for what they had been given, but what the Lord would bless them with as a result of their obedience.

The Greatest Tither

There is a principle in the kingdom of God that a leader never asks anything of those following him that he is not willing to do himself. Jesus demonstrated this law when He washed the disciples' feet and later died on the cross. The King of kings is the greatest servant of all.

God the Father also demonstrated this principle when He gave His only begotten Son, the firstborn and finest, to be the ultimate sacrifice for mankind. This is why Jesus is called the firstfruits of God. God sowed His absolute best into the earth. The Father died to His Son, and the Son died to the Father. Like a seed, Jesus was buried in the earth, rose from the dead in newness of life, and became the firstfruits of all those who were to be born again through His resurrection. We have come into the kingdom of God because of Him.

Jesus Christ is the firstfruits, and God the Father is the greatest tither of all!

But now is Christ risen from the dead, and become the firstfruits of them that slept.
First Corinthians 15:20

Jesus was the guarantee that all those who would call upon His name and be saved, would be good. It was no accident Jesus was resurrected on the Jewish day of Firstfruits.

Jesus was resurrected on the first day of the week of Unleavened Bread, which was called Firstfruits. The Sabbath was the last day of the week, and Firstfruits was the first day of the week.

71

When Jesus came out of the grave that Sunday morning and presented Himself to God the Father, there were priests going through the fields, gathering the first ripened fruit. As they gathered the first and best, they would come to the end of the field and wave the grain, the firstfruits, before the Lord.

As the priests waved their offering before the Lord, Jesus was resurrected and being waved before God the Father as His firstfruits.

The priests proceeded to beat the grain and grind it into flour, which was made into dough and rolled into two rolls. The two rolls were braided together and baked. Then it was eaten at the Feast of Pentecost.

On the Day of Pentecost two loaves, Jews and Gentiles, were braided together for the first time in the upper room. A brand new loaf was created — the church of the Lord Jesus Christ!

The firstfruits is very significant to God. Through Jesus Christ, the firstfruits given by God Himself, a whole new dispensation had begun. The church was now being formed. The Bible says in Ephesians 2:14, "For he is our peace, who hath made both [Jews and Gentiles] one, and hath broken down the middle wall of partition between us." The wall dividing Jews and Gentiles was laid flat. The crushing of Jesus' life, made Jews and Gentiles into one loaf, one body, one church.

After all this, God turns to His children and says, "If I could raise Jesus from the dead and start the church by giving of My firstfruits, don't you think I can do the same thing with the firstfruits of your income?" (author's paraphrase). What can God do when we take our hands off the tithe and totally devote it to Him?

God will take our gift and make something incredible out of it! Just like His firstfruits, Jesus, brought forth many sons and daughters of God, the tithe and offerings we give to God will bring an outpouring of blessings back into our life.

Reversing the Earth's Curse

At the Feast of Firstfruits, the Jews presented every type of crop and animal to the Lord. God wanted these separated to Him at the time of Firstfruits, so people would declare God was Lord over the *ground*. In Genesis 3:17-19 we discover why it is important to God that His people declare Him Lord over the earth.

And unto Adam he said, Because thou hast hearkened unto the voice of thy wife, and hast eaten of the tree, of which I commanded thee, saying, Thou shalt not eat of it: cursed is the ground for thy sake; in sorrow shalt thou eat of it all the days of thy life;

Thorns also and thistles shall it bring forth to thee; and thou shalt eat the herb of the field;

In the sweat of thy face shalt thou eat bread, till thou return unto the ground; for out of it wast thou taken: for dust thou art, and unto dust shalt thou return.

Adam, who had been given dominion over the earth by God, obeyed Satan instead of God. In doing this, not only was the earth cursed, but Satan became Adam's new lord. Because Adam still had dominion over the earth, Satan replaced God as the lord of the earth.

In the world we live in today, God is the God of the universe, but Satan is the lord over the earth. Because of this, the ground is cursed, which means everything produced from the ground is cursed. This not only includes crops, but the bodies of man and animals.

God told Adam he would still have dominion over the earth, but because his master was now Satan, he would have to struggle to succeed in the earth.

However, God gave Adam the key to reducing the struggle and guaranteeing success. God told Adam to take the firstfruits that come from the ground, and *cherem* (devote, separate, consecrate, dedicate) it to Him. Then it would become holy and bring forth abundance in his life.

When we give to God, our gift becomes holy and guarantees that everything will come back in abundance.

A Strange Story

There is a strange little story Jesus told in Luke 16:1-8:

> And he said also unto his disciples, There was a certain rich man, which had a steward; and the same was accused unto him that he had wasted his goods.
>
> And he called him, and said unto him, How is it that I hear this of thee? give an account of thy stewardship; for thou mayest be no longer steward.
>
> Then the steward said within himself, What shall I do? for my lord taketh away from me the stewardship: I cannot dig; to beg I am ashamed.
>
> I am resolved what to do, that, when I am put out of the stewardship, they may receive me into their houses.
>
> So he called every one of his lord's debtors unto him, and said unto the first, How much owest thou unto my lord?
>
> And he said, An hundred measures of oil. And he said unto him, Take thy bill, and sit down quickly, and write fifty.
>
> Then said he to another, And how much owest thou? And he said, An hundred measures of wheat. And he said unto him, Take thy bill, and write fourscore.
>
> And the lord commended the unjust steward, because he had done wisely: for the children of this world are in their generation wiser than the children of light.

When we finish reading this parable, we want to say, "That was strange! Why is that parable in there?" Here's a man who knew he was about to get fired, but he still had control over his master's money. He was the accountant, but he hadn't been doing a very good job, so he went around to all his master's clients and cut their bill in half.

What he was trying to do was to buy favor with his master's clients. Then, as soon as he was fired he could go to the clients and say, "Hey, remember me? I cut your bill in half, so why don't you hire me?" He was planning for the future in order to get another job after he was fired. Even though the boss didn't like what the servant did, he had this to say about him: "You sure are smart — in the wrong way — but you are smart."

Jesus is not saying to double-cross your boss if he's about to fire you! The point of this whole parable is simply that sometimes people in the world are smarter than the children of God. Unbelievers sit around and plan how they can be secure financially. They know how the business world operates. It's amazing how somebody can get born again, spirit-filled, and become financially ignorant!

Although the Lord tells us many unbelievers are smarter when it comes to money, He goes on to say, "Let me tell you how to be smarter than the world."

Making Friends

And I say unto you, Make to yourselves friends of the mammon of unrighteousness; that, when ye fail, they may receive you into everlasting habitations.
Luke 16:9

The money you receive is not blessed of God. It came out of the world's system. It is the mammon of unrighteousness. There's no such thing as righteous money and unrighteous money. It's all unrighteous money.

There are Christians who won't buy a certain product because they found out somebody in the organization is a member of a cult. They won't stay at a certain chain of hotels because that chain is owned by another cult. The truth is, after awhile you couldn't live anywhere, go anywhere, or eat and drink anything, because everyone out there is somehow connected with Satan's world!

Wherever we go, whatever we do, and whatever goes in our body — we need to thank God and sanctify it with prayer. It may have come to us through the hands of unbelievers, but we can pray over it, and it becomes holy.

When we tithe and give offerings into the work of the kingdom of God, we are making friends with the mammon of unrighteousness, which is the money of the world's system. With the tithes and offerings given from our income, many will be born again. Then, "when ye fail" (when you go to heaven) these friends will escort you into the everlasting kingdom of God.

When we sow our finances into the kingdom of God and let go of them, God puts them to work through the hands of His children. Gospel tracts are published, Bibles and teaching materials are distributed, and missionaries are sent out to preach the gospel. Our money is now gathering friends across the globe, who we will meet as friends in heaven.

The Firstfruits of the Spirit

For we know that the whole creation groaneth and travaileth in pain together until now.

And not only they, but ourselves also, which have the firstfruits of the Spirit, even we ourselves groan within ourselves, waiting for the adoption, to wit, the redemption of our body.

Romans 8:22,23

The whole creation groans because everything is under the curse of Adam's sin. The first thing the Holy Spirit gives us is the new birth. Anything after that is wonderful, but it can't compare to the new birth. Likewise, any blessing after the tithe is wonderful, but it can't compare to the tithe.

Because we have the firstfruits of the Holy Spirit living in us, we groan within ourselves waiting for the redemption of our body. We have the guarantee of a great crop coming later, and that is our bodies being resurrected.

We guarantee the rest of our income is going to grow through the years by giving our tithe to the Lord! We will see overflowing abundance come into our life, and we will meet a multitude of friends in heaven who came into the kingdom of God from the firstfruits we sowed!

We will all stand redeemed in spirit, soul, and body, because God gave His Son Jesus Christ.

As men and women, we still have dominion over the earth when we receive Jesus Christ as our Lord and Savior and bring the firstfruits of all our income to God. Jesus redeemed us from the curse of the law when he died on the cross, and Satan, the devourer, is rebuked for our sake. (Galatians 3:13; Malachi 3:9-11)

6

Seedtime and Harvest

There is a story about a husband and wife who had been married for a number of years. He was driving down the road, and she was sitting by the window on the passenger side. Neither one of them had said anything for quite some time. She was looking out the window thinking about her concerns, and he was watching the road thinking about his concerns.

Suddenly a car went around them wildly. A boy was driving with his arms around his girlfriend, and she was practically sitting on his lap. When the older woman saw this, tears came to her eyes. She said, "Honey, did you see that?"

Her husband said, "Yeah."

She said, "Remember when we used to do that?"

"Yeah."

"Whatever happened?"

And he said to his wife, "I haven't moved."

Sometimes we look at the Lord and say, "Lord, remember how close we used to be and how we used to talk all the time?"

And the Lord would say, "Yeah."

"Whatever happened, Lord?"

"I never moved."

God doesn't move! We're the ones who move. God never changes; we change.

We can all remember times in our life when we couldn't wait to get to church. We were excited to worship the Lord and hear the Word of God. Giving to God was a highlight of the service. Now we may look at our life and see how much has changed. We are the one who has changed! God never changes.

The First Law of Prosperity

God gave the following verse of Scripture to Noah after the flood had ended, and he and his family had come out of the ark onto dry land. They were now going to repopulate the earth, but the earth had changed. It wasn't the same as it was before the flood, and that frightened them. God comforted them with the following promise:

While the earth remaineth, seedtime and harvest, and cold and heat, and summer and winter, and day and night shall not cease.

Genesis 8:22

God is telling Noah although things around him have changed, there is one thing that is constant: As long as the earth exists, there will be seasons, day and night, cold and heat, and seedtime and harvest.

As long as this earth remains, no matter what we face in life, we can count on these four things. Satan can't change them; demons can't change them; the world can't change them; man can't change them; and we can't change them because God declared it to be so.

Throughout the Old Testament there were terrible times of drought, and such things as a locust invasion in the book of Joel. When the people went out to harvest the crops, four swarms of locusts descended, one after another. The first swarm ate the fruit, the next ate the stalk, the third one ate the stubble, and the last one went down into the ground and ate the roots. The people thought their lives were over, but afterwards seedtime and harvest come again. It always comes back!

We're living in a time when the earth is going through some major changes. Every day the news bombards us with how we are the ones causing it. We are messing up the environment, polluting the air, and causing global warming. In the book of Ecclesiastes, Solomon pointed out that the earth goes through cycles. The sun comes up and the sun goes down. The waves come in and the waves go out. Everything operates in cycles. Without this knowledge of God's Word, catastrophes or changes in the earth occur and people panic. But believers can have confidence that as long as the earth exists there will always be seasons, day and night, cold and heat, and seedtime and harvest.

One thing we often forget is that the earth is not fragile. God created the earth, and He did a good job. In fact, the Bible makes it clear that man will never destroy the earth. In the end, God will destroy it and give us a brand new earth.

Man keeps saying we've done something wrong to upset the delicate balance of nature, but nature is not fragile. All we have to do to prove this is go out to a concrete parking lot and look at the plants that are growing in the middle of it, or visit the site of a devastating forest fire a year ago. We can see the law of seedtime and harvest in action.

There is something about catastrophe that causes nature to come back stronger than it was before. We can't wipe it out. These things have been happening for centuries.

The Natural Mirrors the Spiritual

The same law governs spiritual seedtime and harvest. When we make the commitment to give the firstfruits of our increase to the Lord, trials, are going to come against us, because the devil doesn't want us to succeed. That's when we look him straight in the eye and declare, "As long as the earth exists there will always be seedtime and harvest. My business may be struggling right now, but this is only temporary. God said He would pour abundance into my life, and God's Word always prevails!"

We have to make up our mind that tithing is not a one-time "let's see if it works" deal. If that is our attitude, when the attack of the enemy comes, we will go back to living in the land of just enough, or even allow the bondage of Egypt to take hold of our finances again.

We may say to ourselves, "Oh, my, inflation may be coming. I had better hold onto my tithe."

"My children are going to college in a few years. I can't afford to give to the Lord right now."

"The company has lost too many contracts this year and there is talk of laying off some employees. There's too much going on here for me to give my money to God."

"What if someone in my family would get very sick? The insurance would never cover everything, and that kind of catastrophe would break me. I'll just have to pass on this ten percent stuff until I can really afford it."

Trials are a part of life, and Satan does all he can to increase them even more in our life when we dedicate ourselves to tithe into God's kingdom. His purpose is to get us to stop giving. He wants to prevent us from receiving the abundance God has for us. He knows when we receive that abundance we can give even more into the preaching of the gospel and be a testimony to others to do the same.

When we are attacked in our finances remember *the attack is a temporary condition.* The permanent condition is no matter what happens, there will be seedtime and harvest. God will give us wisdom and strength to go through the attacks, and because we stand firm in our giving, we will come out even better than before.

What Have You Got To Lose?

Whether or not we participate in God's plan by tithing doesn't stop the plan of God, but our participation is what causes us to receive His blessings in that plan.

For we can do nothing against the truth, but for the truth.

Second Corinthians 13:8

This Scripture says you can do nothing against the Word of God, only for it. If we rebel against God and step out of His plan for our life because the pressure is too great, don't think God stops because we stopped. He keeps right on going! When we repent, and get back in His plan, we will find His plan didn't stop just because we did. Because our heart is right, He will restore us completely.

Maybe it has been a number of years since you have tithed, or maybe you have never tithed. Believe it or not, God didn't stop in His tracks, heaven didn't fall apart, and Jesus didn't fall off the throne because you weren't participating in His plan of prosperity for your life. Start participating right now and watch your life change dramatically!

I met a man in the airport who had made the commitment to tithe many years ago. He said his abundance didn't come in overnight, but progressively over time. At first a little bit started coming in, then a little more, but he continued to tithe and give offerings. Today he owns and manages his own business and has a tremendous income.

Another man I talked to said he began tithing and his income increased very quickly, so he decided to tithe out of his business profit. He said, "I figured if it worked for me, it would work for my business." His business began to grow, and he discovered that the same blessings were poured out on his business. He remarked, "The ten percent I set aside for God became holy and dedicated to Him, because I realized that the purpose of my business was not just to benefit me, but to help finance the kingdom of God."

R. G. LeTourneau is the man who invented the heavy earth-moving equipment eventually bought by Caterpillar. He began giving ten percent to God, and by the time he was older he was giving ninety percent to God and keeping the ten percent for his own expenses! He commented even the ten percent was more than he could use for the rest of his life. His giving to the Lord sent missionaries around the world to spread the gospel of Jesus Christ.

The most exciting testimonies we have received at our church are from those who are on fixed incomes. They decided to give Jesus the firstfruits of their income, and God began to show them that "fixed" was not a word in His vocabulary!

There is no possible way we could lose by giving into the kingdom of God. Natural principles speak of spiritual principles, and God's principles of prosperity will work despite natural circumstances.

Jesus told us in the parable of the sower and the seed that trials and troubles come to steal the Word from our heart and pressure us into not obeying God's Word. (See Matthew 13, Mark 4, and Luke 8.) But what happens after the troubles and the trials are over?

Storms in the natural realm or the spiritual realm only last for a while. If we stand firm and obey the Word of God in the tithe, we will always prosper — especially after a great trial!

Once we have made the commitment to tithe, we shouldn't let anything cause us to stop trusting in God's promises. We must allow nothing to steal our joy and ultimately cause us to give up. Remember the attacks are temporary, but God's Word will stand forever. If we continue on in faith, we will succeed.

Speaking Up for Prosperity

What shall we then say to these things? If God be for us, who can be against us?

Romans 8:31

What shall we then *say* to these things? "You mean we speak to things?" Yes! We speak to things. Jesus spoke to a fig tree and it withered and died. He spoke to the stormy weather and it became calm. He rebuked sickness and commanded it to leave and people were healed.

If we can rebuke sickness like Jesus did, then apparently sickness can hear. We don't talk to things that can't hear. Jesus talked to the fig tree because the fig tree could hear. And now the same principle comes to us. "What shall we then *say* to these *things?*" We say to *things*, "If God before us, who can be against us?"

He that spared not his own Son, but delivered him up for us all, how shall he not with him also freely give us all things?

Who shall lay any thing to the charge of God's elect? It is God that justifieth.

Who is he that condemneth? It is Christ that died, yea rather, that is risen again, who is even at the right hand of God, who also maketh intercession for us.

Who shall separate us from the love of Christ? shall tribulation, or distress, or persecution, or famine, or nakedness, or peril, or sword?

Romans 8:32-35

We've been born again, and we have the firstfruits of the Spirit, so who is it who comes against us? When trials come against us, we should be *speaking* to those things! We shouldn't allow the trials of life to overcome us.

We have a stabilizer inside us to keep us on course no matter how the winds blow for the moment. We know the wind can't last forever, and as soon as it is over, we will be right back on our way. We won't give up, because greater is the Word of God in us than the storms coming against us in the world.

Nothing can separate us from the love of Christ. Therefore, we can speak to peril, distress, persecution, physical problems, pressure, anger, and any kind of lack. "Bank account, if God be for me you cannot be against me. Lack of money, you're temporary, but God's Word is eternal. Financial pressure, you can't last, because nothing can separate me from the love of Christ. And when all this is over, I'm still going to be standing; there will still be seedtime and harvest, and God's abundance will be mine."

> As it is written, For thy sake we are killed all the day long; we are accounted as sheep for the slaughter.
> Nay, in all these things we are more than conquerors through him that loved us.
> For I am persuaded, that neither death, nor life, nor angels, nor principalities, nor powers, nor things present, nor things to come,
> Nor height, nor depth, nor any other creature, shall be able to separate us from the love of God, which is in Christ Jesus our Lord.
> **Romans 8:36-39**

Our abundance will come to us first of all good measure, then pressed down, next shaken together, and finally running over. (Luke 6:38.) Your return can be thirty-, sixty-, then one hundred-fold. (Mark 4:20)

Along the way, there are temporary setbacks. Sometimes we move faster, sometimes slower, but no storm can ever cause God's kingdom to quit working. Seedtime and harvest remain! God placed this unchangeable law of prosperity in the earth to enable you to continue to succeed, no matter what comes against you!

7
Priming the Pump

Several years ago I heard a popular folk song about a man who was going through the desert and was extremely thirsty. He came across a water pump and found a little container of water sitting next to it. The container had a lid on it with a note attached. It said, "In this jar is water to prime the pump. Don't drink this water! If you will use this water to prime the pump, you will have more water than you can use."

There was water in abundance below the ground, but because this pump sat for so long, it dried out and wouldn't work by itself. It needed just enough water to prime it. The song talked of how the man looked at the water and then looked at the pump and said, "Do I trust the person who wrote this note? If I pour the water into the pump, begin pumping, and nothing happens, I've lost a drink of water." But he went ahead, swallowed his fears, and poured the water down the pump.

The man began to pump and pump. For the longest time nothing happened and all his fears began to say, "See, you should have drunk the water instead of pouring it in there." Just then he heard a rumbling sound come from under the ground. Suddenly, water began gushing out! There was so much water that he drank and drank and rolled around in it. Then he filled up his canteens and was careful to leave the little container — full of water — with the note attached for the next person who needed to prime the pump.

Your tithe is the container of water which will prime the pump of your prosperity, allowing the abundance and success God has for you to come gushing into your life. You may have been drinking your tithe, settling for that little container of just enough for today. Maybe you have not been taught about God's plan for prosperity, or perhaps you are afraid to use the tithe to prime the pump in order to receive what God wants to give you — more than you can think of or imagine!

Obeying in Faith

What God ministered to me on the airplane coming home from Latvia was this: "My people are not holding back the tithe because of rebellion, but out of fear. They are just afraid to step out in faith and obey My Word." If believers can overcome their fear by understanding the love God has for them and how He desires to bless them, they will give to the Lord and find out their fears were unfounded. Their fears come from Satan, who wants to keep them from receiving God's blessings.

Why did Jesus ask the servants at the wedding in Cana to fill the pots with water? I don't know, but if He told me to fill a pot with water, or with anything else, I would do it.

Why do we have to anoint people with oil? Why didn't God instruct us to anoint with water, wine, or something else? Think about it — we could be anointing with wine, drinking water at communion, and baptizing new converts in oil!

Before Jesus turned the water in the pots to wine, Mary told the servants, "Whatever He says to you, do it" (John 2:5, author's paraphrase). This is for us today! When we obey God, His blessings will begin to pour into our lives.

Why are we to give ten percent? The ten percent is simply a matter of obedience, not percentage. If God had commanded eight percent or twelve percent, it would still be a matter of obeying His Word. God is looking for those who will show their love for Him by obeying Him.

If ye love me, keep my commandments.

John 14:15

Jesus answered and said unto him, If a man love me, he will keep my words: and my Father will love him, and we will come unto him, and make our abode with him.

John 14:23

Often we read the Bible and wonder why God said certain things. In some cases, God does not want us to know *why* He said it. He just wants us to obey Him in faith. He is simply looking for obedience.

God was looking for obedience in Abraham when He told him to offer his son Isaac as a sacrifice to Him. (See Genesis 22:2) God didn't intend for Abraham to kill his son. He just wanted to see if Abraham would be obedient.

Abraham looked at his body, which was practically dead, and the deadness of Sarah's womb, but he staggered not at the promise of God that they would have a son. (Romans 4:19-21) Abraham decided to trust God, and Isaac was the result. In the same way, we need to look at the promises of God and overcome our fears about tithing. When we obey and trust Him by tithing, incredible miracles can take place in our lives.

If ye be willing and obedient, ye shall eat the good of the land.

Isaiah 1:19

The Challenge

I challenge you now to let this next week be the week you move from the land of just enough into the land of abundance. In the following pages I have listed a Scripture for each day of the week and a confession. Meditate on the

Scripture for that day. Write it down and carry it with you. Take it out whenever you can and read and meditate on it during the day.

Ask the Holy Spirit to reveal to you all the fears and excuses you have used for not giving to the Lord regularly. Use each Scripture to confront your fears and excuses and expose them for the lies they are. Then choose to believe God's Word over the lies.

On the practical side, as you are confessing and meditating on these Scriptures, sit down and thoroughly examine your financial state. Look at your budget and allow the Holy Spirit to guide you concerning it. If you have never had a budget, it is never too late to start. There is nothing wrong with seeking good Christian financial counseling if you need help in this area. Many people simply have never learned how to handle their money.

When you have gathered all the facts, prayerfully set your budget and include ten percent for your tithe. If you can go over ten percent, even better.

For six days, Monday through Saturday, prepare yourself to take Jericho by marching around the wall of your fear and excuses. Every time you have a thought of fear or an excuse rises up about why you should not give to God, break the power of the enemy by speaking the Scripture for that day. Set your heart and mind on God's Word.

By Sunday, all of your excuses and your fears are going to fall flat, just as the great wall of Jericho crashed to the ground. This will be the day you will look back on as a turning point in your financial life. It will also be a turning point in your relationship with God. You will draw closer to Him and trust Him more than you ever have, because you are giving Him first place in your finances. From this point on, every time you get a paycheck, you will automatically and joyfully give the firstfruits to the Lord.